W9-AIU-620

Also by Shannon Hale, Dean Hale,
and Nathan Hale

Rapunzel's Revenge

Also by Shannon Hale

THE BOOKS OF BAYERN
The Goose Girl
Enna Burning
River Secrets
Forest Born

Princess Academy
Book of a Thousand Days

For adults
Austenland
The Actor and the Housewife

Also by Nathan Hale

The Devil You Know
Yellowbelly and Plum Go to School
Balloon on the Moon (illustrations)
The Dinosaurs' Night Before Christmas (illustrations)
Animal House (illustrations)

Published by Bloomsbury U.S.A. Children's Books
175 Fifth Avenue, New York, New York 10010

Library of Congress Cataloging-in-Publication Data
Hale, Shannon.
Calamity Jack / Shannon and Dean Hale ; illustrated by Nathan Hale.—1st U.S. ed.
p. cm.
Summary: In this graphic novel interpretation of "Jack and the beanstalk,"
Jack is a born schemer who climbs a magical beanstalk in the hope of exacting justice
from a mean giant and gaining a fortune for his widowed mother, aided by some friends.
ISBN-13: 978-1-59990-076-6 • ISBN-10: 1-59990-076-9 (hardcover)
ISBN-13: 978-1-59990-373-6 • ISBN-10: 1-59990-373-3 (paperback)
1. Graphic novels. [1. Graphic novels. 2. Giants—Fiction. 3. Characters in literature—Fiction.]
I. Hale, Dean. II. Hale, Nathan, ill. III. Jack and the beanstalk. English. IV. Title.
PZ7.7.H35Cal 2010 [Fic]—dc22 2008041332

Book design by Nathan Hale
Balloons and lettering by Melinda Hale
HushHush and Pulp Fiction fonts by Comicraft
Color mapping by Yodit Solomon, Melinda Hale, Lindsay Hale, Layna Connors, and Lauren Widtfeldt

First U.S. Edition January 2010
Printed in China by South China Printing Co. Ltd., Dongguan City, Guangdong
2 4 6 8 10 9 7 5 3 1 (hardcover)
2 4 6 8 10 9 7 5 3 1 (paperback)

All papers used by Bloomsbury U.S.A. are natural, recyclable products
made from wood grown in well-managed forests. The manufacturing processes
conform to the environmental regulations of the country of origin.

For Max and Maggie,
the best teammates a couple of schemers
could ever hope for.

—S. H. AND D. H.

To Greg, Riley, and Rebekah.
Three in-laws, three outlaws.

And with thanks to Shannon and Dean—
no relation, but a lot of admiration.

—N. J. H.

Part 1: THE BEANSTALK BONANZA
I think of myself as a criminal mastermind...
...with an unfortunate amount of bad luck.

I was born to scheme.
32 Jack

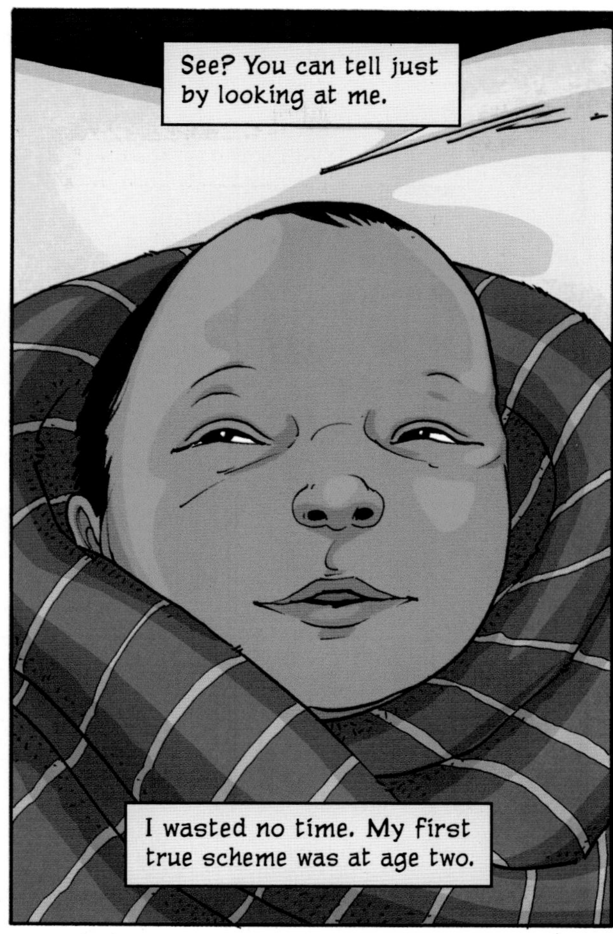
See? You can tell just by looking at me.
I wasted no time. My first true scheme was at age two.

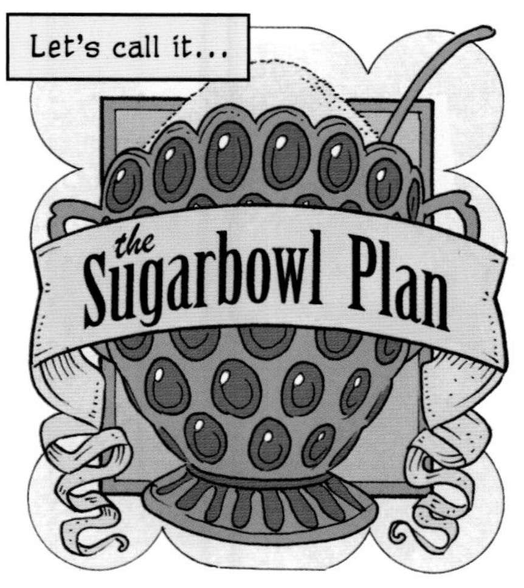
Let's call it...
the Sugarbowl Plan

I'd see something I wanted...
...and my mind couldn't help figuring out how to get it.

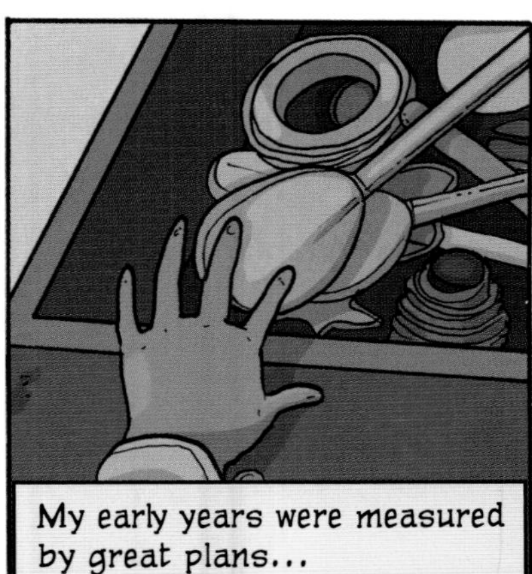
My early years were measured by great plans...

...and unexpected consequences.

Skipping ahead to my school years, we'll call this stunt:
THE GREAT SANDWICH CAPER

TRIP
WIRE
Now, when I say "unexpected consequences..."

...I'm not suggesting my plans didn't work.

They worked! They did!

But you can't plan for everything.

Right?

THE
GROCERY
JOB

Of course, the key to the success of any plan is to get the right people involved, on both sides.
The takers...

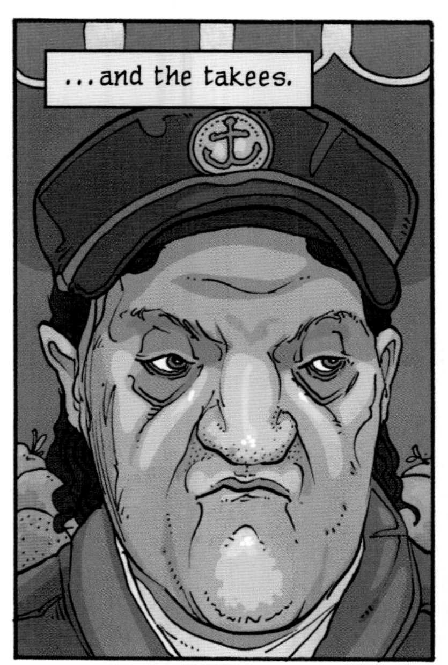
...and the takees.

5¢
DOZEN
BUS

THE
Purloined
PIG

Picking the right chump is vital.

THE CANE MUTINY

And we got pretty good at picking chumps out of a crowd.

THE ICE-CREAM CON

More and more, the "we" became me and Prudence, my favorite partner.

I don't know that I ever thought twice about the folks we swindled.
ONE, PLEASE.

WHAT HORROR!

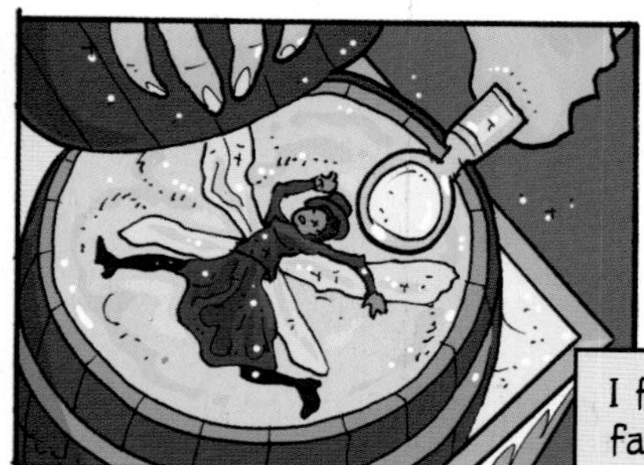

POLICE! HE'S SERVING *PIXIE* ICE!
I'M OUT OF HERE!
I figured, if they were dumb enough to fall for it, then they deserved to lose.

And no harm done. Right?

The
Failed
Flamingo
Filching

Some of our adventures were downright risky...
MONKEY HOUSE
...but I felt invincible in my poppa's cowhide jacket.

It was the only thing of his we didn't hock after he died of the fever.

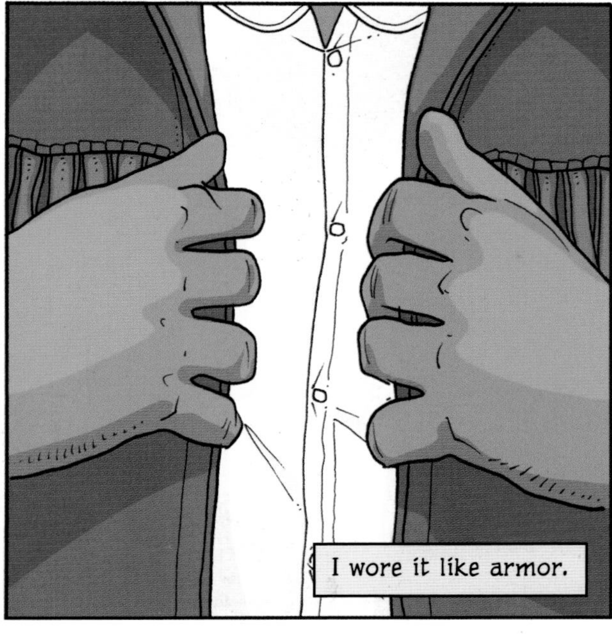
I wore it like armor.

MAUDE'S
MAUDE'S
BAKERY & CAFE
BAKERY
I mostly tried to keep my shenanigans from my momma.

She had enough to worry about.
HEY! YOU DIDN'T PAY FOR LUNCH YET!

FOR THAT HASH? YOU SHOULD BE PAYING ME, COOKIE.
She took care of me, half the neighborhood, and a few stray animals besides.

GET BACK HERE, YOU HOBGOBLIN!
HA!

THIRD FREELOADER THIS WEEK. DON'T KNOW HOW I'M GOING TO AFFORD FIXING THAT OVEN.

But folk disrespecting Momma? Well, that chapped my hide.

So I devised:
The Bowler Hat Heist

This wasn't just about making sport of someone I didn't like or scoring a bit of glory. Now I was feeling the rush of justice.

I felt sure I'd found my calling.

SWIPE

Momma didn't seem pleased to share the spoils.

The Fat Banker Fiasco

But I'd had a taste of justice now, and I began to set my sights higher.

FLIP

WHOOOOOOA!

What if I could scheme my way into *real* money, enough so Momma wouldn't have to sell the bakery?

She'd understand then, right? She might even be proud.

But there were always those...

...unexpected consequences.

Prudence was game for whatever I could think up, so long as she got her part of the loot. Never knew a pixie with such an appetite for hats.

Giant.

Big business boss.

Filthy rich with his fingers in a lot of political pies.

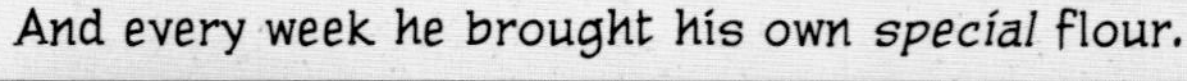
And every week he brought his own *special* flour.

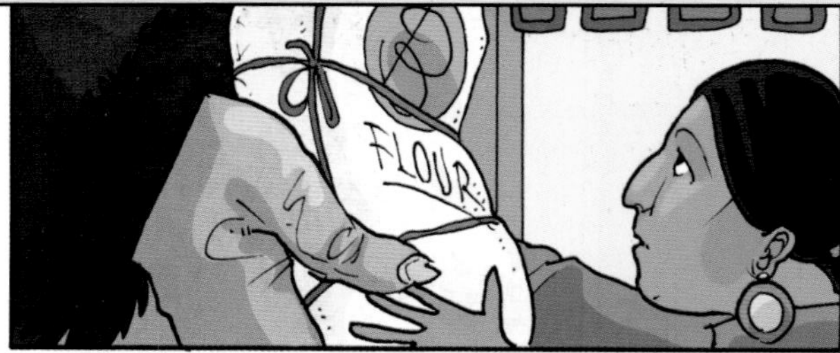
FLOUR

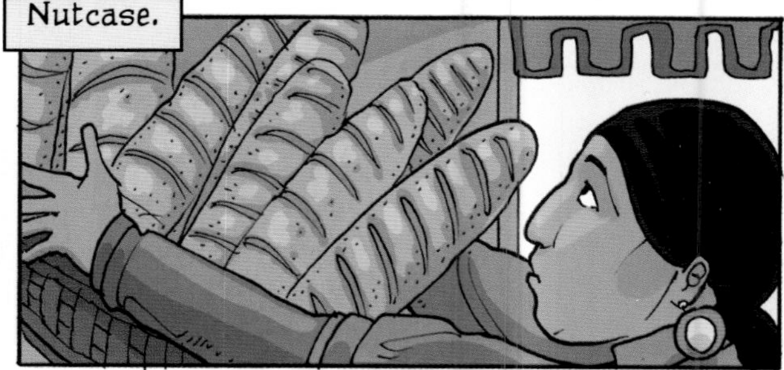
Nutcase.

Something about him gave me the creeps.

CRACK

YOU'LL NEED TO PAY FOR THAT.

I knew just what to do.

The Blunderboar Business

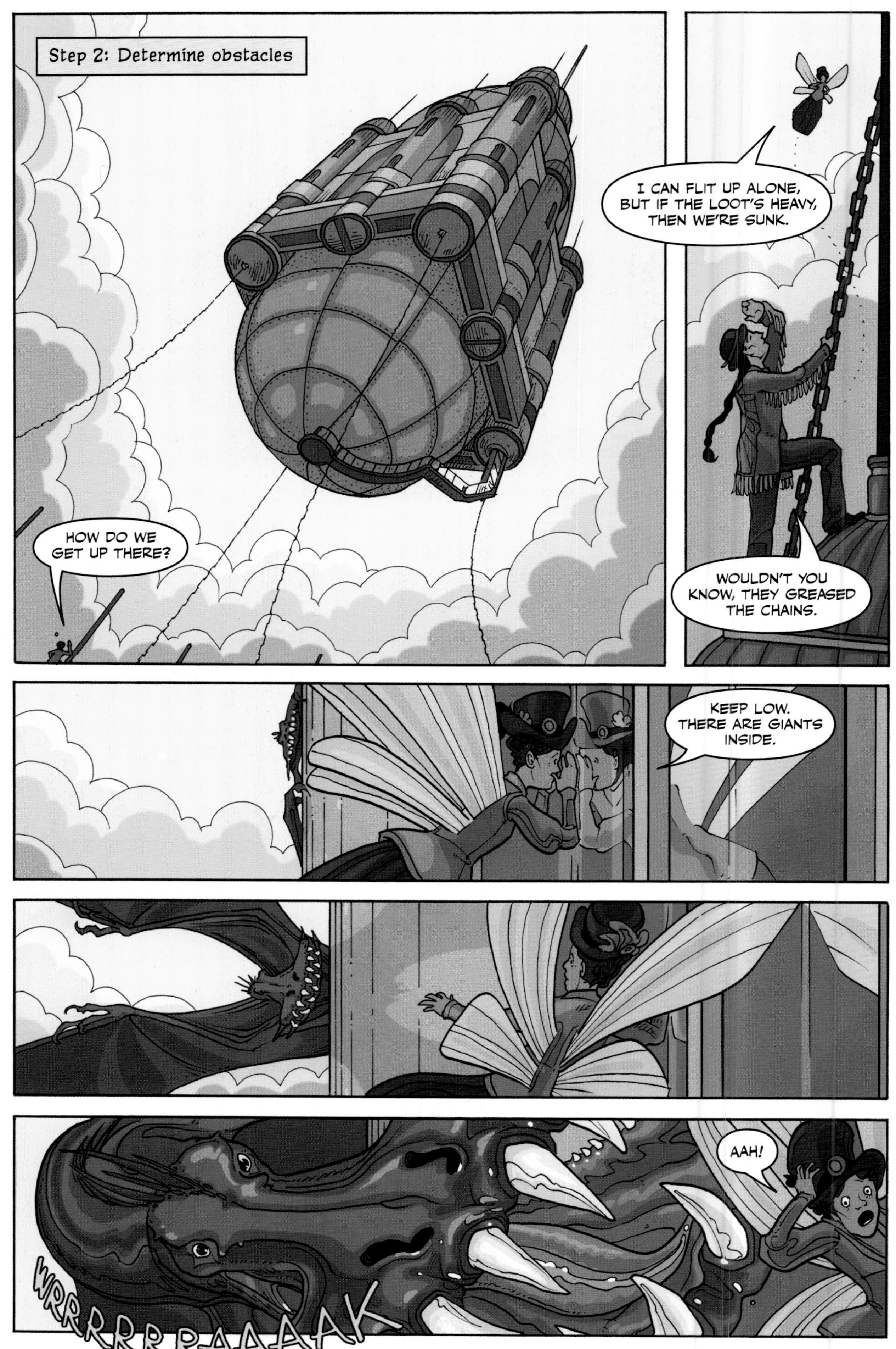

Step 2: Determine obstacles
HOW DO WE GET UP THERE?
I CAN FLIT UP ALONE, BUT IF THE LOOT'S HEAVY, THEN WE'RE SUNK.
WOULDN'T YOU KNOW, THEY GREASED THE CHAINS.
KEEP LOW. THERE ARE GIANTS INSIDE.
AAH!
WRRRRRRRAAAAAK

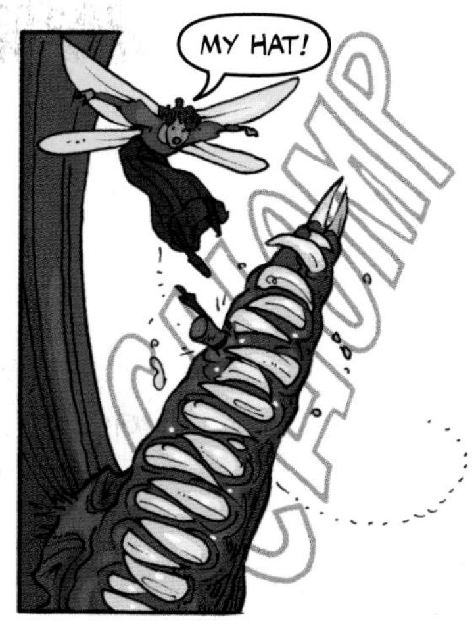

Some fancy folk had guard beasts on their roofs to keep birds and nosy flying folk at a distance. None were so deadly as a jabberwock.

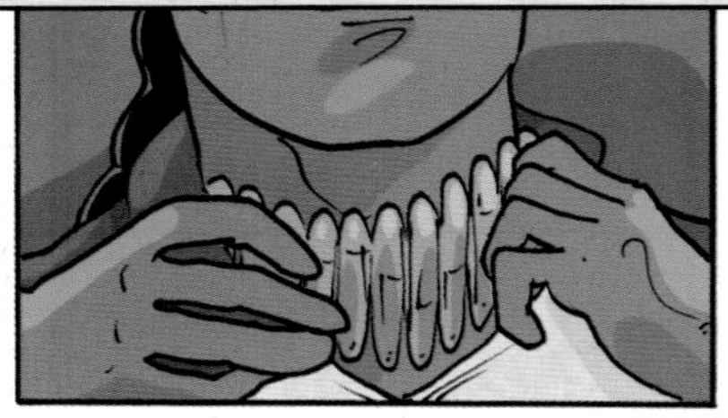

Step 3: Make the plan

JABBERWOCK RANGE
CHAIN LENGTH?
HOT AIR BALLOON
HARPOON
GIANT KITE
POISONED MEAT?
RISKY

The jabberwock ate anything that flew but didn't bother giants climbing the ladder they sometimes lowered down. So, if we had our own ladder...

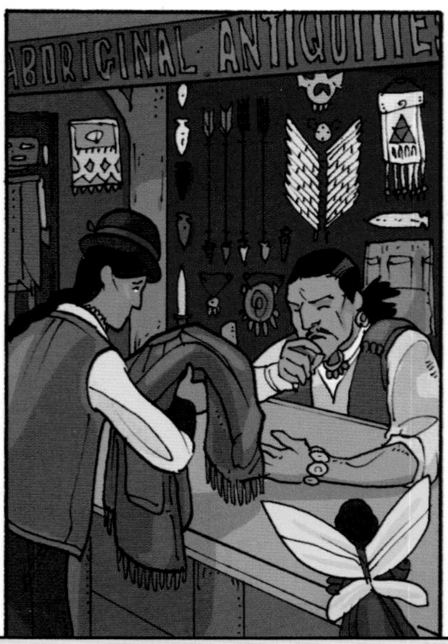

Feeling defenseless without my jacket (not to mention *cold*), I went with Pru in search of something spiffy that'd get us past the jabberwock.
TONICS
'Course, to score the unusual niceties smuggled in from the Old World, you've got to skulk to a market that's just a touch *black*.

Step 4: Gather equipment

I wanted to go from the ground straight up to the floating penthouse...

PFFFFFFFFFFFFFFFFFFFFFFP-POP-POP-POP...
...bypass the jabberwock's perch...
...all without flying.

What could we use as an insanely tall ladder?

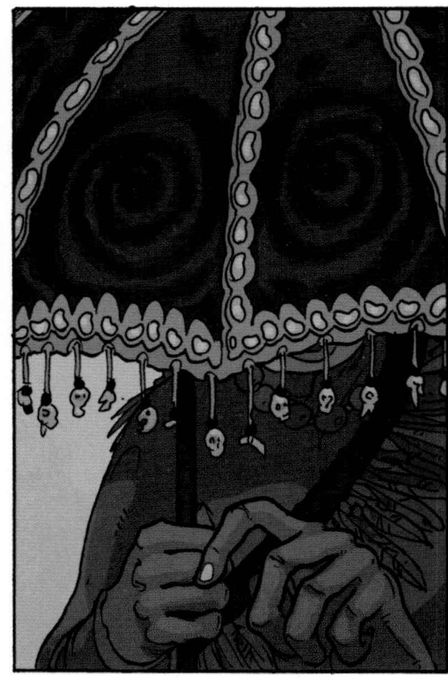

SN4P
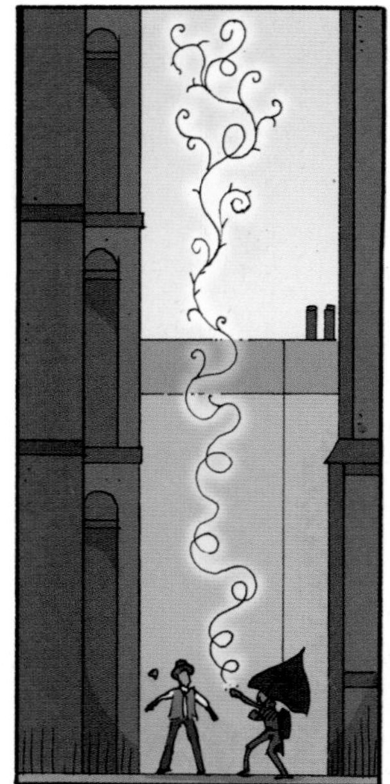

SHAKE SHAKE

If those beans grew as fast and tall as promised...

SNAP

SNAP
SNAP
SNAP

SNAP
POP

I NEVER DID TRUST VEGETABLES.

DOGGONE IT, WE'VE BEEN HOODWINKED! NOW WE'LL HAVE TO GET OUR HANDS ON MORE DOUGH TO BUY SOMETHING ELSE.

COO! COO! COO!

Lousy, useless beans! A powerful ache in my gut told me I'd lost my poppa's jacket for nothing.

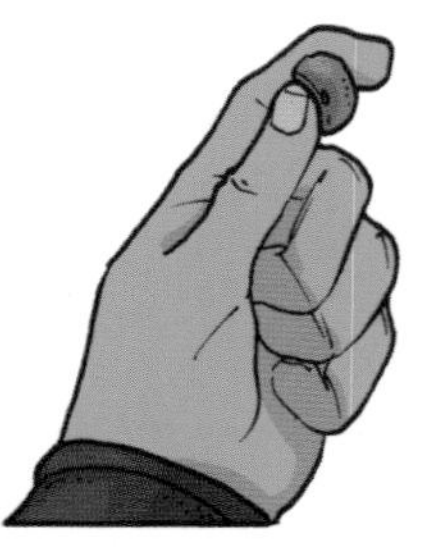
I kept one, just to remind me not to be stupid and trust magic again.

That night, I returned late from an unsuccessful pursuit of an illicit financial opportunity.

WELL, IF THAT DON'T BEAT ALL...

Step 5: See the plan through
I was afraid Prudence would be sore, but I couldn't spare the time to go find her.
Those giants could have discovered the beanstalk at any moment. I had to act quickly.

YEESH.

DON'T LOOK, JACK. JUST LEAP.

AII...

AAH, AAH, AAH...

MR. JABBERS

I'd climbed past the beast and gained the floating penthouse. Luck was mine.

BLUNDERBOAR, SIR, THE MEN ARE READY TO ATTACH THE OMNIPHONE PIPING IN THE PENTHOUSE.

THIS WRETCHED GOOSE IS BEING UNCOOPERATIVE WITH ITS ALLEGED GOLDEN EGGS.

MAY AS WELL GO HAVE A LOOK.

GOLDEN EGGS, EH? THAT'LL DO.

SQUAWK!
SHH.

...YOU KNOW HOW BLUNDERBOAR IS...

WON'T ALLOW HIS PRECIOUS THINGS TO BE UNGUARDED FOR A MINUTE.

TIFFANY, THAT YOU? YOU SEEN MY SHOWER CAP?

SQUAWK?
WHAT WAS THAT NOISE?
JUST LUMPY HOLLERING AGAIN.

HEY, YOU TRY SHOWERING WITHOUT GETTING YOUR HAIR WET.

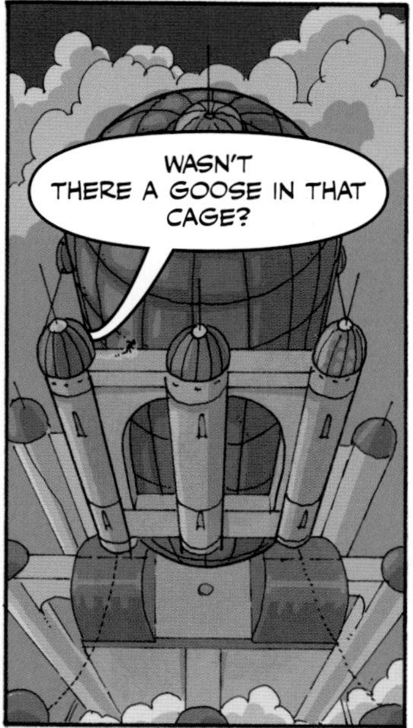
WASN'T THERE A GOOSE IN THAT CAGE?

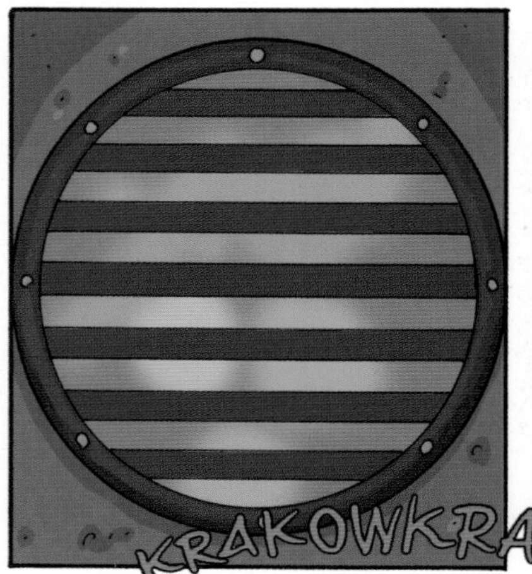

KRAKOWKRAKOWKRAKOWK

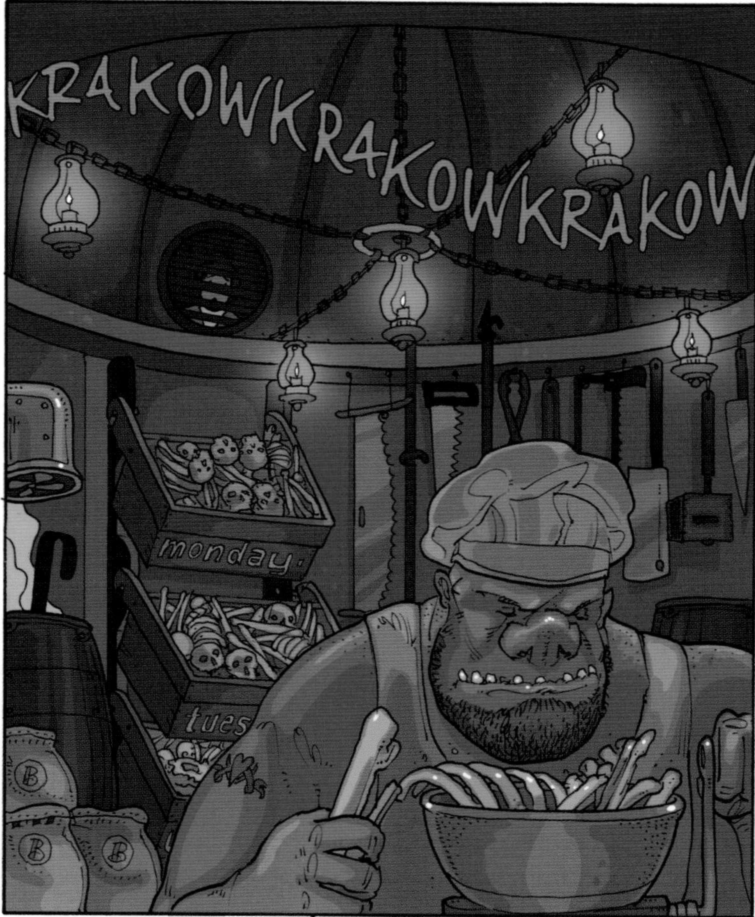
KRAKOWKRAKOWKRAKOW
monday
tues

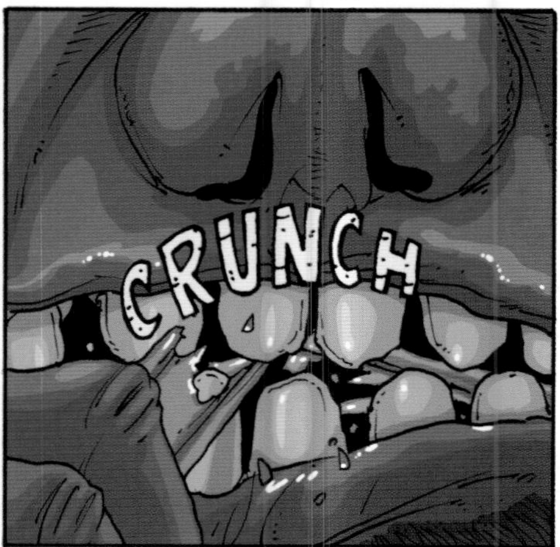
CRUNCH

KRAKOWKRAKOW

IF THAT GOOSE MANAGES TO FLY OFF THE ZEPPELIN AND GETS EATEN BY MR. JABBERS, BLUNDERBOAR WILL SQUEEZE OUR EYEBALLS FOR JUICE.
GOOD POINT. I'LL GO REEL IN THE 'WOCK, JUST IN CASE.

SQUAWK!
DO YOU WANT TO BE BONE BREAD? SO SHH ALREADY!

CLANG
URK...

HHHHU!
KRUMP

SQUAWK!
WHA-
AAH.
NO.

AAH.

KICK

CLANG
NO.
SNIP

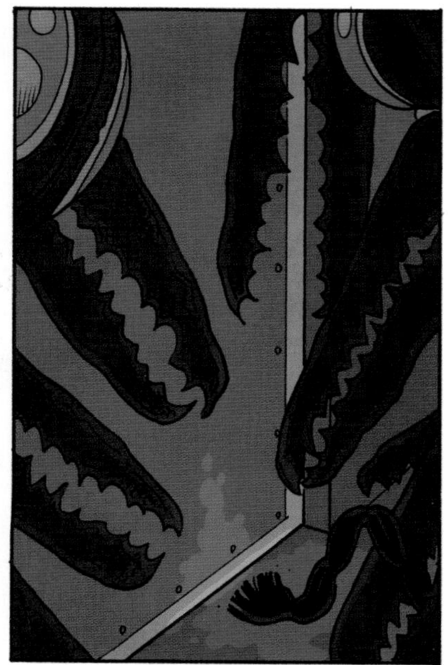

WAAAAAAAA

AAAAAA!
MR. JABBERS
WHUMP

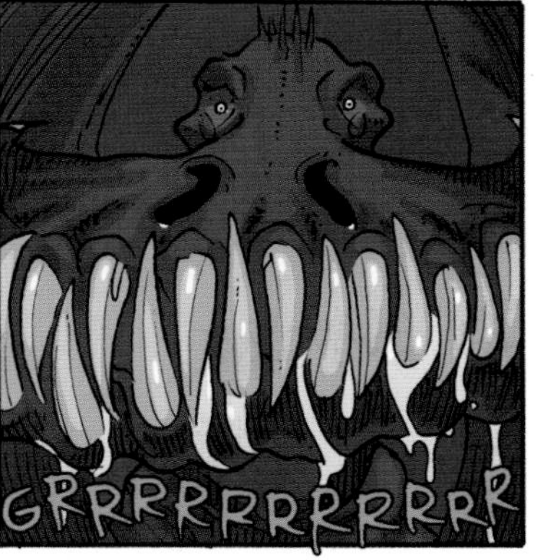
GRRRRRRRRRRR

WRRAAAAAK

CHOMP

AAAAKRAAAK

...CAN'T FIND THAT GOOSE.
I THOUGHT I HEARD SOMETHING OVER HERE.

HAS THAT BIG PLANT ALWAYS BEEN THERE?

I'M NOT GONNA MAKE IT, I'M NOT GONNA MAKE IT...
MAYBE MR. B IS STARTING A GARDEN. REMINDS ME OF THE GIANT ORCHARDS OF...WAIT, DO YOU SMELL A HUMAN?

OOOF!

WHOA!
SQUAWK!

SQUAWK!

And so I had to hop from rooftop to rooftop, hunting down the goose I'd only just stolen.
All night long.

No rest for the wicked, Momma would say.
SQUAWK!

GOTCHA!

Finally got home near dawn, wondering how I was ever going to sleep again after what I'd seen in Blunderboar's penthouse, when—
CREEEEEEEEAK

SIP
AAAAA
ERIK!
AAAAAAAAA
UH...

CRASH
AAAAAA

YOU!

UH...
DRIP

DON'T MOVE!

Things looked a mite rickety at the tenement.
RRRRRRRRRRRR
THAT'S EVERYONE...
CREEEEEEEEE
...AND JUST IN–

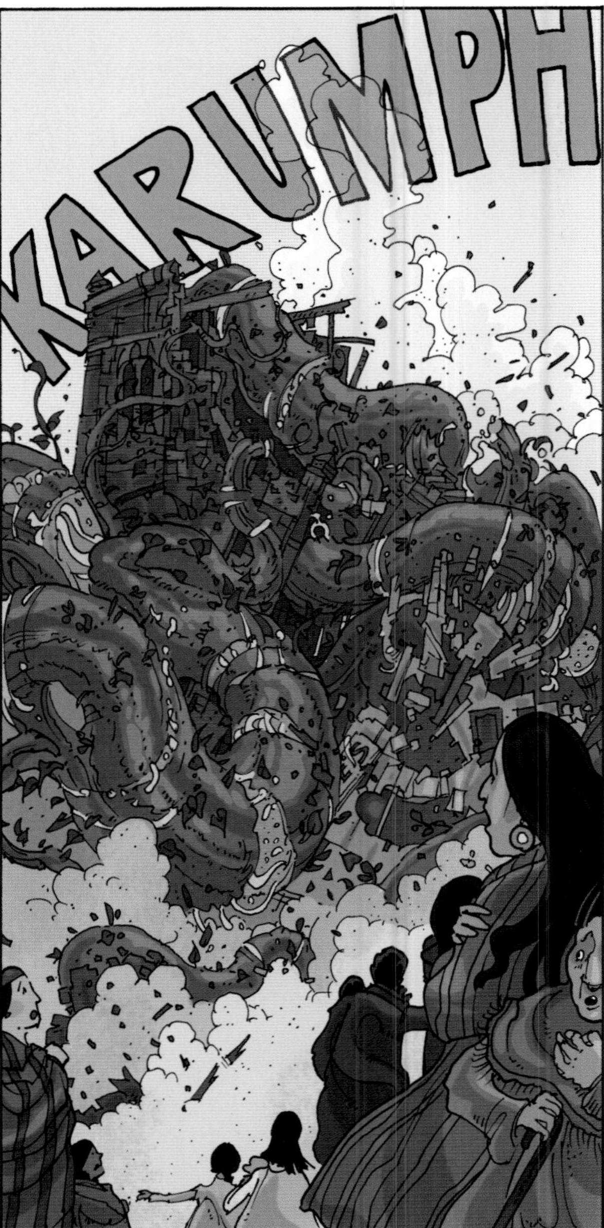
KARUMPH

MOMMA!
YOU'RE ALL RIGHT? YOU DIDN'T GET HURT?

THIS WAS YOU, WASN'T IT?
ME? I DIDN'T–

DON'T YOU STAND IN FRONT OF ME WITH OUR HOME AND BAKERY A HEAP OF BRICKS, NOT EVEN THE TINTYPE OF YOUR FATHER SAVED, AND LIE TO ME...

I'M SORRY, MOMMA.

I WAS JUST TRYING TO... I MESSED UP AGAIN, BUT I'LL FIX IT ALL.
I'LL BUILD US A NEW ONE, I'LL–
ENOUGH, JACK.

BUT THIS TIME I REALLY HAVE A WAY TO MAKE LOTS OF GOLD FAST.
I MEAN, YOU TRUST ME, RIGHT? THAT'S WHY YOU GAVE ME THIS...

I THOUGHT IT'D HELP YOU REMEMBER YOUR ROOTS, TO TRY TO BE *GOOD* FOR ONCE!
INSTEAD YOU LIE AND SCHEME AND DESTROY EVERYTHING, EVERYTHING... I CAN'T TALK TO YOU RIGHT NOW.
JUST GO.

JUST GO.

WHERE IS THE DOOMED BOY WHO KILLED ONE OF MY GIANTS?
And so I went.

I figured she'd be better off without me, and with Blunderboar's giants on the lookout, there didn't seem to be much good in sticking around.
I hopped the iron horse headed Out West and didn't get off until we stopped somewhere I'd never heard of.

GOTHEL'S REACH
TICKETS
EMERALD
My plan was to hide from the giants, wait for Goldy to lay some eggs, then head back to make things up with Momma—build the nicest tenement and bakery in all the New World Territories. Show her I could be good.

Then things got complicated.

But sometimes that's a good thing.

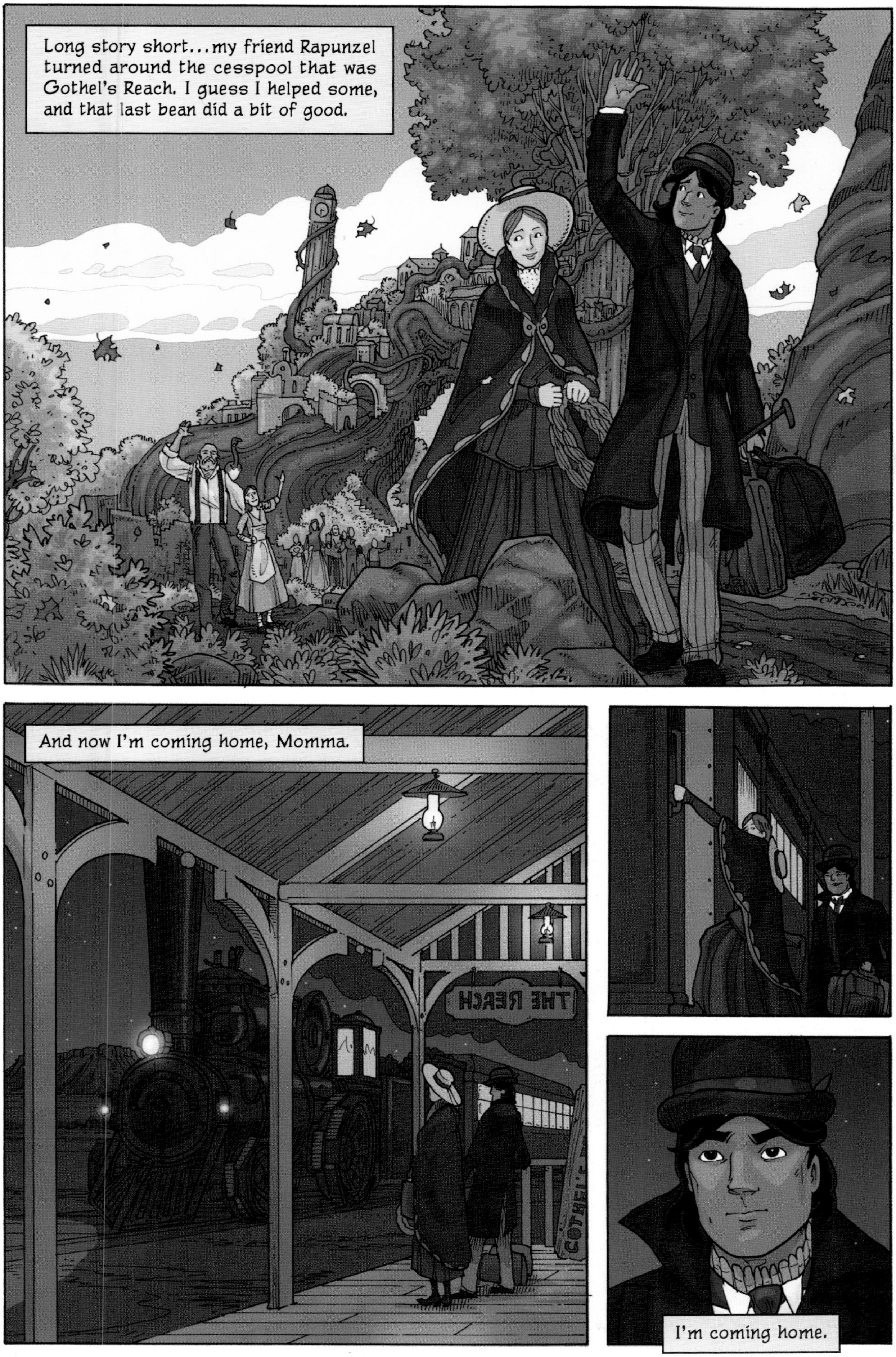

Long story short...my friend Rapunzel turned around the cesspool that was Gothel's Reach. I guess I helped some, and that last bean did a bit of good.

Part 2: Jack the Giant Killer

I also happened to notice that she looked pretty good by the light of a kerosene lamp.

Whether we were gaming or resting, eating or gabbing, she kept her braids close at hand in case there was trouble.
I almost had her convinced we were leaving the lawless West behind and heading toward safe civilization when...

CHAKA CHAKA
CHAKA CHAKA

IS THE IRON HORSE SUPPOSED TO DO THAT?
YOU MEAN MAKE THAT OMINOUS SOUND AND LURCH UNPLEASANTLY? I SURE HOPE NOT.
ANT PEOPLE CONTINUE ASSAULT ON SHYPORT

THUD

SCRAPE

AAAH!

RRIIIPP
IT'S THEM!

SKRRCC
IT'S *THEM!*
SAVE US! SAVE US!

SKReeeeeeee
WHO'S THEM? WHAT IS IT?

THE ANT PEOPLE! THEY'RE HERE!

THE ANT...
GREAT.

EVERYBODY BACK TO THE CABOOSE!

COME ON NOW. GIT!

UUH...

SOME HELP HERE!

CREEEAAAK
UNCOUPLER

KRANG
UNCOUPLER

CHAKA CHAK

CHAKA CHAK

SKREEEEEEEE

ANT PEOPLE!

ANT PEOPLE!
CLICK
CLICK
BLAM
BLAM
PTING
TING
PTING
BBLAM
SKReeeeeeeeeeeeeeeeeeeeeeeeeeeeeeeeeeeeeeeeeeee
GRAB HOLD!

EEEEEE!

...EEEEEE...

...EEEEEE...

...EEEEEE...

BLAM
BLAM

RIP

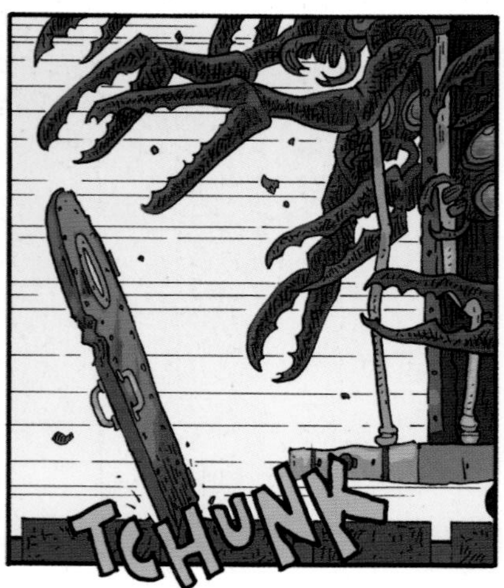
TCHUNK

POW

SCREEEEEEEEECH

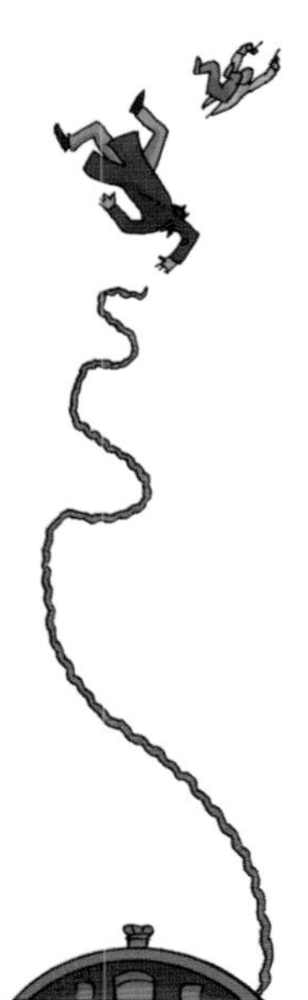

WHAM

THANKS FOR BREAKING MY FALL.
UH-HUH. BUT NEXT TIME, *YOU* GET TO BREAK *MY* FALL.
DEAL.

THUD
OOOOF

SURE ENOUGH, NOTHIN' BUT NICE, SAFE CIVILIZATION OUT HERE.

YEAH...

When we caught up with the rest of the train, the monsters were gone.
NEVER FEAR, SMALL FOLK!

BLUNDERBOAR AND COMPANY DISCOVERED THE ANT PEOPLE'S NEFARIOUS PLOT TO DESTROY THIS IRON HORSE. WE HAVE CHASED THEM BACK INTO THEIR DANK HOLES.

HOORAY!
PRAISE BE!
I SWEAR, THOSE ANT PEOPLE WOULD'VE BURNED SHYPORT TO THE GROUND LONG AGO IF NOT FOR BLUNDERBOAR.

BLUNDERBOAR?
ISN'T THAT THE ONE YOU—
YEAH, THE VERY SAME GIANT. LET'S MAKE OURSELVES SCARCE.

HEY...WEREN'T THERE BOXES IN HERE BEFORE?

MAYBE THEY FELL OUT WHEN THE IRON HORSE DERAILED.
BUT THIS CAR STAYED UPRIGHT.

YOU ARE SAFE NOW!

ALL ABOARD FOR SHYPORT!

WHAT A BUNCH OF MORONS.
HEH. YOU GOT THAT RIGHT.

DID THEY...
DID THEY JUST CALL US A BUNCH OF MORONS?
YEAH, I WONDER WHAT THEY MEANT...

BESIDES THAT WE'RE A BUNCH OF MORONS?
CLAKITY-CLAKITY-CLAKITY
RIGHT. BESIDES THAT.

THIS IS MY AUNT GWEN'S FLAT. IF SHE'S STILL HERE, SHE'LL LEND US A CORNER.
KEEP OUT

AAAH!

SLAM
UH, AUNT GWEN? IT'S ME, JACK. CAN WE COME IN?

...HAVE YOU SEEN THEM, JACKIE? HAVE YOU SEEN THEM?

SEEN WHAT?

WHERE ARE YOU?

THE *ANTS!*

BUGS THAT WALK LIKE MEN! ANT PEOPLE, JACKIE! ANT *PEOPLE!*
WHUH?
YAH!

PEOPLE GO MISSING ALL THE TIME. YOU REMEMBER DOBBIN PUTTERKIN, THE DUGGER WITH THE VEGETABLE STAND ON SLIM STREET?
YEAH...

HE WAS EATEN! AND OFFICER GURNEY?

SO–

EATEN!
AND CRAZY OLD PHILOMENA ZEP?

EATEN!!

LISTEN, I JUST SAW MY MOTHER AND I'VE GOT TO–
PSSHT! YOU'VE GOT TO STOP CAUSING TROUBLE FOR HER. BLUNDERBOAR'S LOCKED HER UP TO BAKE HIS BREAD AND NEVER LETS HER OUT WITHOUT A GUARD.
HE'S... HE'S HOLDING HER? THAT SWINDLING, DEEPLY ROTTEN–
SAYS SHE AIN'T GOIN' NOWHERE TILL HE GETS HIS HANDS ON HER MURDEROUS SON.

IF I TURN MYSELF OVER TO HIM, HE'LL LET HER GO?
YOU'RE BAD NEWS, SONNY. NOW OUT BEFORE SOMEONE SEES YOU AND LOCKS ME UP TOO! SHOO!

SLAM
SO...THAT WAS YOUR AUNT, HUH? I COULD SEE THE FAMILY RESEMBLANCE IN HER, UH, NOSE.
YEAH...

HE'S HOLDING HER IN THAT FORTRESS OF A...

PROPERTY FOR LEASE
SPACIOUS ROOMS
NICE VIEW
C'MON, I'VE GOTTA SEE SOMETHING.

I'D WAGER MY GOOSE...

...THAT BLUNDERBOAR'S MADE SOME IMPROVEMENTS IN SECURITY...

...SINCE I WALTZED IN ON A BEANSTALK.

LET'S JUST SEE...

...WHAT THEY MIGHT BE.

CLACK

eeeeee
eeeeeeeeeeeeeeeeeeeeeeeeeeeeee...
eeeeee

eeeeeeeeeeeeeeeee

eeeeee
eeeee
eeeeeeeeeee

NOTHING'S OUT THERE.
I'M REELING THE BROWNIES BACK IN.
eeeeeERK

HIC

SCREAMING BROWNIES. WEAR ALL THE EARMUFFS YOU WANT, THE SOUND GOES RIGHT THROUGH. I ONCE SAW A FELLA FORCE HIMSELF TO ENTER A BUILDING PROTECTED BY JUST ONE SCREAMING BROWNIE. HE MADE IT AS FAR AS THE DOOR BEFORE HE STARTED TO BLEED FROM THE EARS.

AND BLUNDERBOAR HAS DOZENS OF THEM CHAINED IN THOSE CELLS.
CHAINED... THAT'S HORRIBLE! WE'VE GOT TO–

WHAT, BLEED FROM OUR EARS? COOL YOUR HEELS, THEY'RE PROBABLY PAID EMPLOYEES.

PAID TO BE CHAINED UP?
EH, BROWNIES ARE WEIRD THAT WAY. ANYWAY, FIRST PRIORITY IS MY MOTHER. WE CAN LIBERATE THE ALARM SYSTEM LATER.
HMM.
YAH!

WHAT? OH! EW. UM...JACK, CAN THOSE THINGS SEE US?
PROBABLY THE JABBERWOCK CAN.
THE...UH... *BANDERSNATCH,* I DON'T KNOW. IN ANY CASE, IT MIGHT BE A GOOD IDEA TO GET OUT OF SPITTING RANGE.

BANDERSNATCHES SPIT?
WITHOUT GETTING INTO TOO MUCH FLESH-BURNING DETAIL, YEAH, PUNZIE, THEY SPIT.

JACK, THIS PLACE IS INSANE.
YEP. HOME.

EVERYTHING'S JUST DAISY, ISN'T IT?
IT'S NO BOWL OF CHICKEN SOUP, THAT'S FOR SURE. LET'S GET A WIGGLE ON.

MY MOMMA LOOKED SO SAD... SHE'S NOT LIKE THAT. SHE'S FEISTY.
WE'LL GET HER OUT. PICK UP THE PACE THERE.

RAPUNZEL, THERE'S NOWHERE TO GO.

DON'T YOU HAVE ANY FRIENDS?

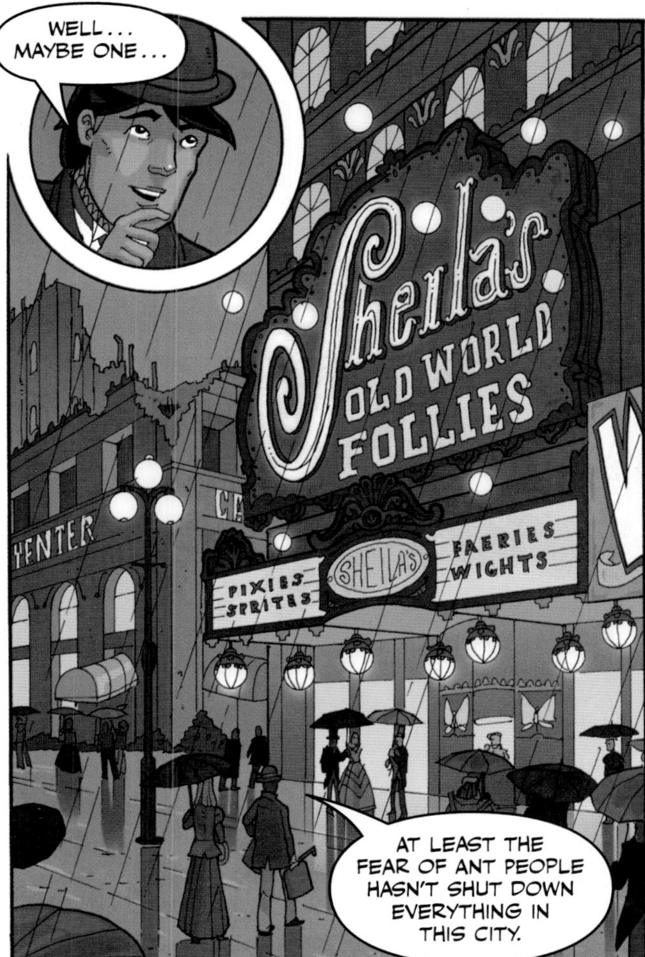
WELL... MAYBE ONE...
Sheila's OLD WORLD FOLLIES
SHEILA'S
PIXIES SPRITES
FAERIES WIGHTS
AT LEAST THE FEAR OF ANT PEOPLE HASN'T SHUT DOWN EVERYTHING IN THIS CITY.

STAGE DOOR

THE GAL IN PURPLE ON THE END? THAT'S PRUDENCE. WE USED TO RUN TOGETHER.
RUN?
UH...WORK TOGETHER.
BUT WHAT... WHAT ARE THEY?

PIXIES.

NOW THERE'S THE WIDE-EYED LOOK OF A...
IF YOU SAY "BACKWATER GIRL," I'M GOING TO KICK YOU IN THE SHINS.

BUT WOW. THAT'S...WOW.
SEE? I TOLD YOU THERE WERE WONDERS.
JACKIE! LONG TIME NO SEE, CHIEF.
HIYA PRU,
YOU'RE LOOKIN' SWELL. THIS IS MY FRIEND RAPUNZEL.

WELCOME, HONEY. ANY FRIEND OF JACKIE'S MUST BE A-OK.

DRESSING ROO
HOW'S SCHEMES?
SINCE YOU GHOSTED OFF, MY SALARY HERE HAS BEEN PAYING THE RENT, BUT IT'S NOT NEARLY ENOUGH TO KEEP ME IN HATS.

A MILLION GOLD COINS WOULDN'T BE ENOUGH TO KEEP YOU IN HATS.

HYSTERICAL.
ANYWAY, I'M READY TO GET BACK INTO THE GAME. WHAT'S THE NEW HEIST?

HEIST?
WHAT A SILLY—WHY WOULD I—*AHEM*, PUNZIE AND I ARE TRYING TO LAY LOW. CAN WE SLEEP AT YOUR PLACE TONIGHT?

OPEN
SURE THING, JACKIE, BUT AREN'T YOU DYING TO CRACK OPEN BLUNDERBOAR'S GIANT FLOATING TREASURE HOUSE AND SEE WHAT'S INSIDE?

"CRACK OPEN BLUNDERBOAR'S . . ." HA! YOU ALWAYS WERE A CRACK-UP, PRU.

TEE-HEE! EMPTY YOUR POCKETS, MY PRETTY VICTIMS.

WHUP

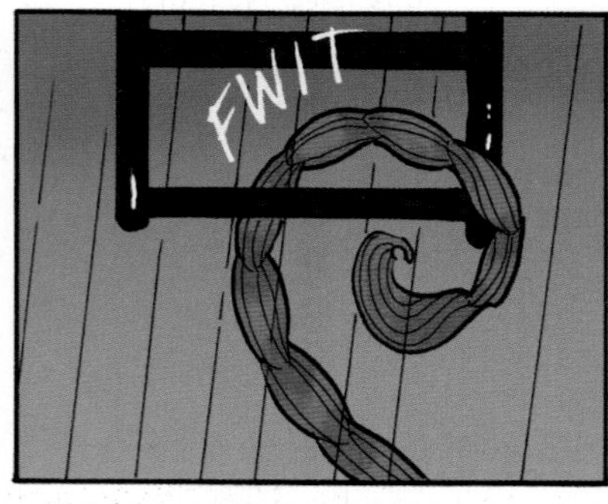
FWIT

CHUNK

GET LOST, NUMBSKULL.
YOU SURE KNOW YOUR WAY AROUND THE STREETS, HONEY.
Isn't she fantastic? I thought about telling her so right then and there, but Rapunzel's not the type of girl who cares about sappy compliments.

NOT REALLY. I'M FROM OUT WEST, BUT BAD GUYS ARE THE SAME NO MATTER WHERE YOU ARE.

I was hoping Prudence would keep her lips buttoned about how I'd been one of those bad guys.

Rapunzel knew I had a sordid past...
...but I'd never offered details on the whole preying-on-the-innocent-for-profit parts. I reckoned if she knew, she'd split and never look back.

We got to Pru's...

...took the visitor's entrance...

...and curled up for the night.

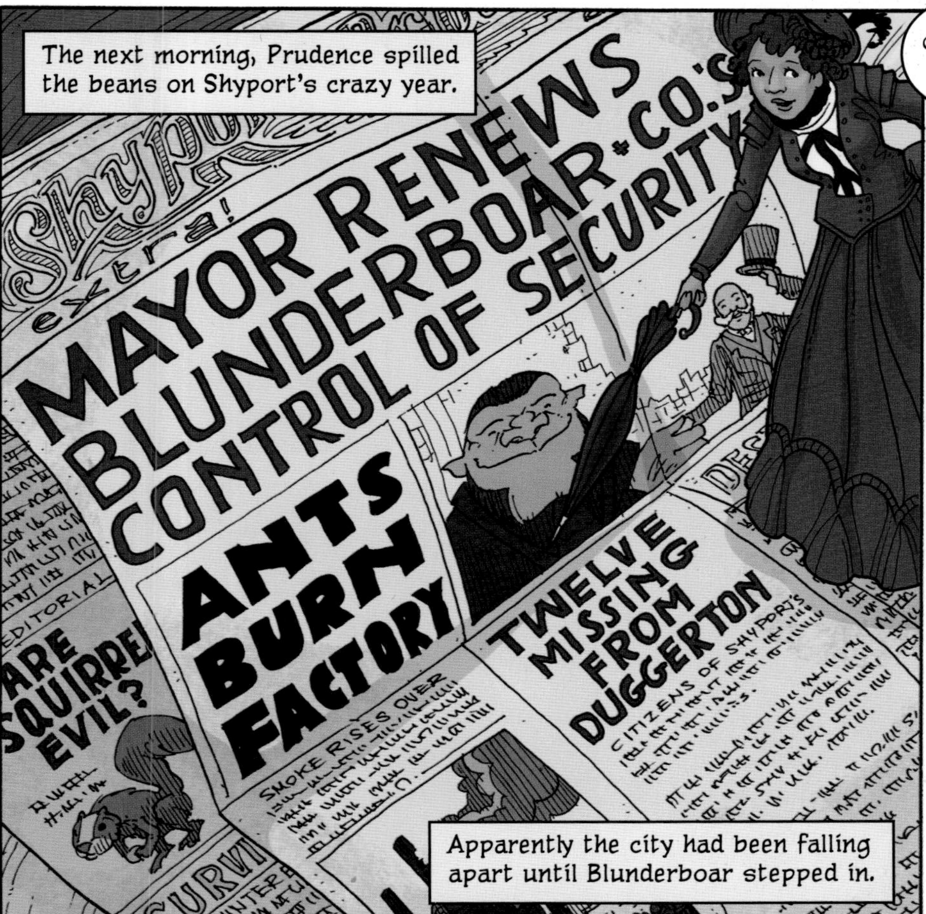
The next morning, Prudence spilled the beans on Shyport's crazy year.
extra!
MAYOR RENEWS BLUNDERBOAR & CO.'S CONTROL OF SECURITY
ANTS BURN FACTORY
TWELVE MISSING FROM DUGGERTON
ARE SQUIRREL EVIL?
SMOKE RISES OVER
CITIZENS OF SHYPORT'S
EDITORIAL
Apparently the city had been falling apart until Blunderboar stepped in.

SO HE'S CONTROLLING THE POLICE FORCE?

HE *IS* THE POLICE FORCE.

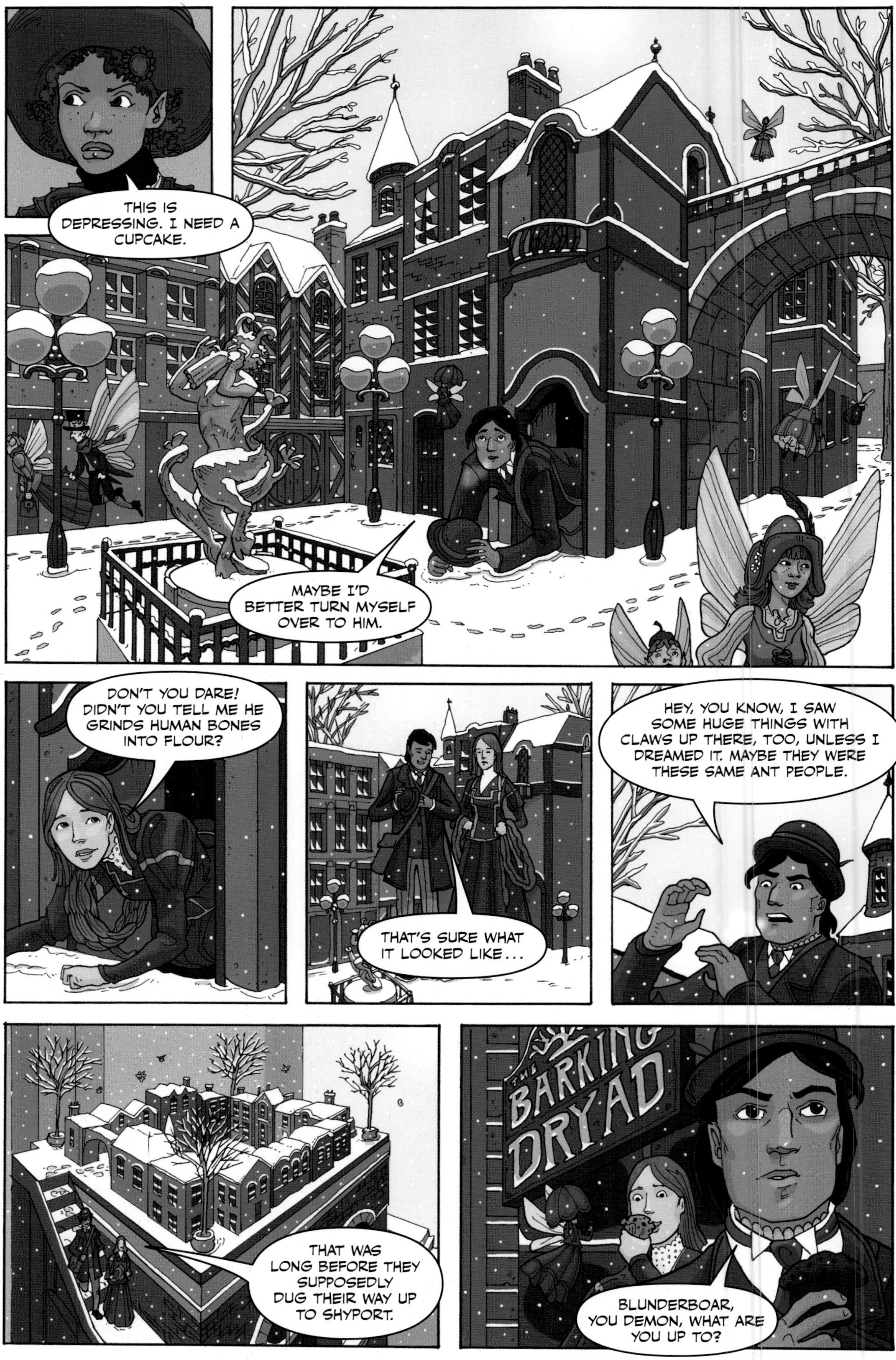

THIS IS DEPRESSING. I NEED A CUPCAKE.

MAYBE I'D BETTER TURN MYSELF OVER TO HIM.

NEWS AGENT
TOBACCO
WE ARE OPEN!
SPARKSMITH PUBLICATION
THE SHYPORT SHEET Tells you the TRUTH!
NEWS FROM ALL FRONTS
SPARKSMITH... THAT WAS THE LABEL ON THOSE CRATES FROM THE IRON HORSE...

...THE ONES THAT WENT MISSING—
A SPARKSMITH PUBLICATION
CONVENIENTLY RIGHT AFTER THE ANT PEOPLE ATTACKED.

HEY, PRU, KNOW WHERE WE CAN FIND THE *SHYPORT SHEET* OFFICE?

WHAT—*ACK!*

MY HAT!
NATIONAL BANK
GET OUT NOW!
CRUNCH
After a brief detour to Pru's for another hat, we made our stealthy way to Turich Street.

WHAT'S THAT NOISE? IS IT ANOTHER SHYPORT WONDER?
ODORLESS EXCAVATOR
LATRINES EMPTIED
THRUM-THRUM-THRUM-THRUM-THRUM

I'M NOT SURE...

HELP! SOMEONE CALL BLUNDERBOAR! THE ANTS ARE ATTACKING! THE ANTS ARE ATTACKING!
ODORLESS EXCAVATOR
TURICHSTRASSE
THRUM·THRUM·THRUM·THRUM·THRUM·THRUM·THRUM·THRUM

THRUM·THRUM·THRUM·THRUM·THRUM·THRUM·THRUM

ANT PEOPLE, YOU WILL TERRORIZE THIS CITY NO MORE! SHYPORT IS UNDER THE PROTECTION OF BLUNDERBOAR! WE'LL GIVE YOU ONE CHANCE TODAY—RETURN TO YOUR UNDERGROUND PITS OR FACE OUR FURY.
SECURITY
ANTI-ANT PATROL
32

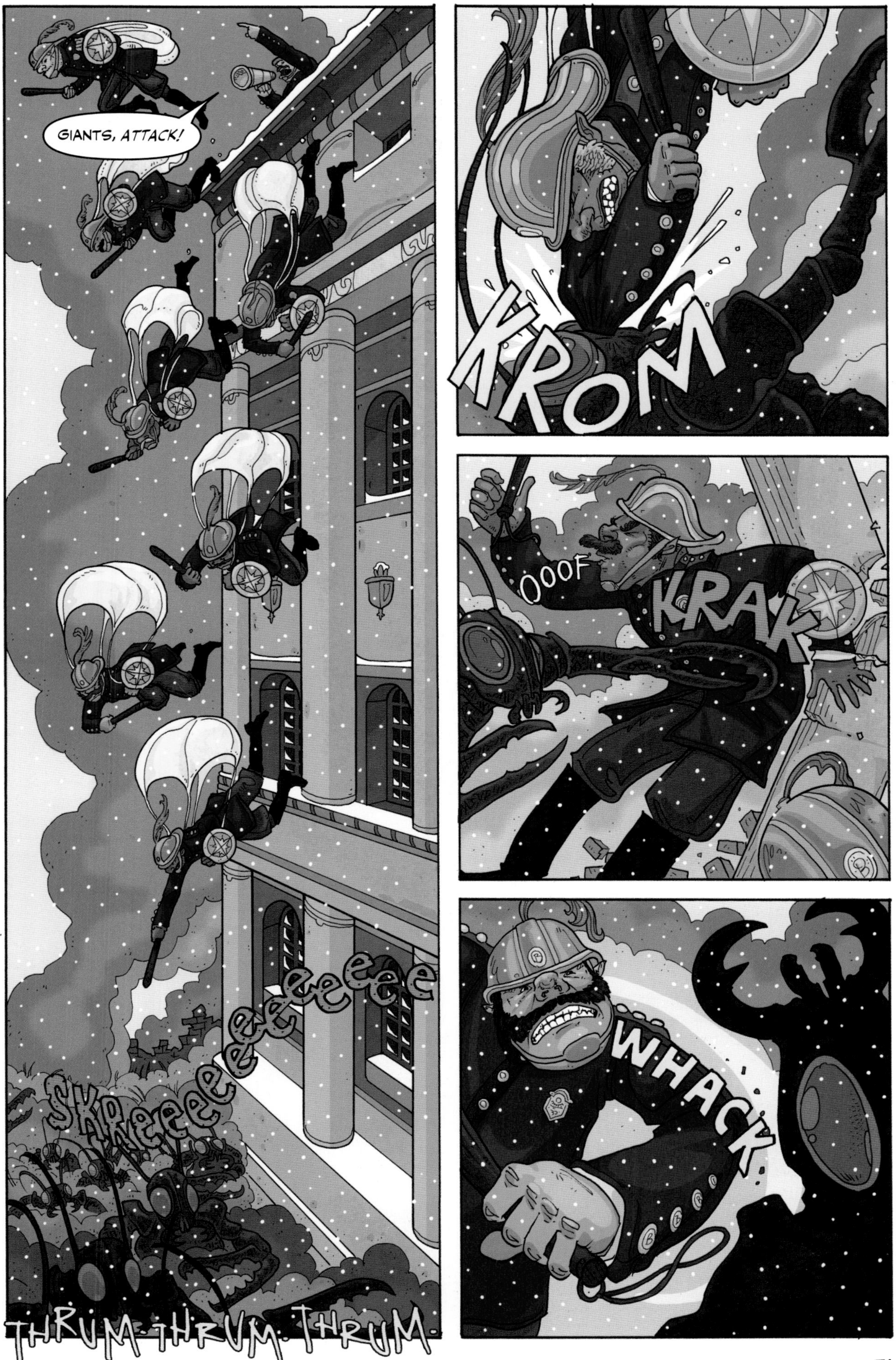

GIANTS, ATTACK!

SKREEEEEEEEEEEEEE

THRUM THRUM THRUM

I TELL YOU, I WILL NOT BE BULLIED, YOU BULLYING BULLIES, YOU!
I WILL NOT–

SPARKSMITH
INDUSTRIES
I SAY, I WON'T–

I'M NOT MOVING! I WILL PROTECT THIS NEWSPAPER WITH MY LAST BREATH.

HE'S GOING TO GET HIMSELF KILLED!
WHAT A NUTJOB.
COME ON, WE'VE GOT TO SAVE HIM.
UM.

C'MON!
RIGHT. OKAY. SAVE HIM.

SHAME ON YOU, GIANTS! DOUBLE SHAME!
I SPECULATED THAT THESE BATTLES PURPOSELY OCCUR NEAR BLUNDERBOAR'S COMPETITORS,
AND TODAY CONFIRMS IT!
I'LL GO FRONT PAGE, I WILL!
SIX MONTHS AGO, ANT PEOPLE DEMOLISH THE URBAN OMNIPHONE CENTER!
LAST MONTH, ANT PEOPLE BURN DOWN THE *SHYPORT GAZETTE*!
WELL, MY POPPA'S BUSINESS WON'T CRUMBLE SO EASILY!

MOVE!

JACK!!

OOF!

KRUSH

AAH, IT'S BREAKING . . . GET READY . . . IT'S YOUR TURN . . .
MY TURN FOR WHAT?

SPANG

AAK!
WHUMP
OW.

TO BREAK MY FALL. WHAT A GENTLEMAN.
MY PLEASURE.

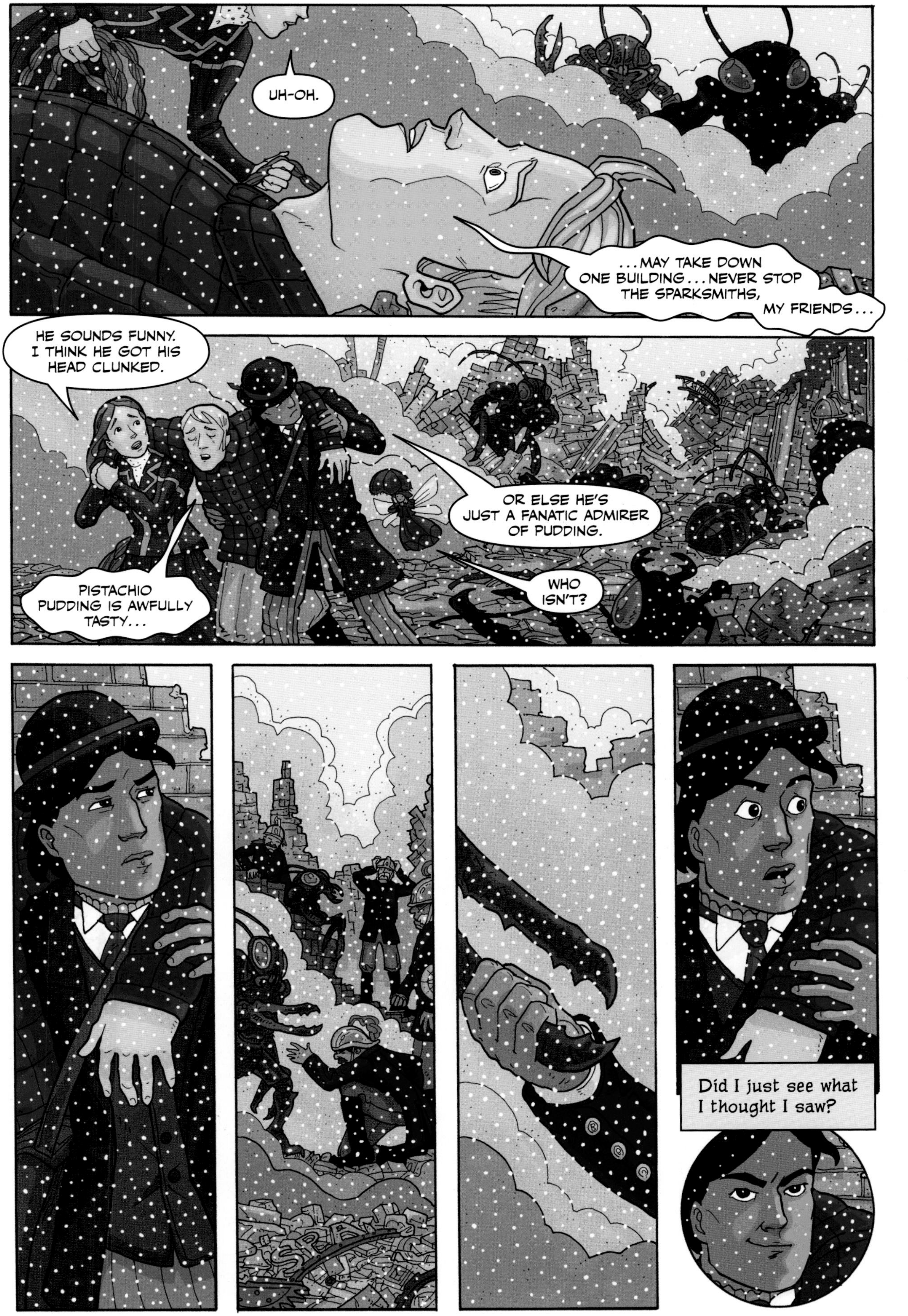

UH-OH.
...MAY TAKE DOWN ONE BUILDING... NEVER STOP THE SPARKSMITHS, MY FRIENDS...

HE SOUNDS FUNNY. I THINK HE GOT HIS HEAD CLUNKED.
PISTACHIO PUDDING IS AWFULLY TASTY...
OR ELSE HE'S JUST A FANATIC ADMIRER OF PUDDING.
WHO ISN'T?

Part 3: To Catch an Ant

BLUNDERBOAR CHOOSES TO FIGHT THE ANT PEOPLE WHEREVER HE'D LIKE SOME DAMAGE DONE, THAT'S WHAT I SAY.

ACTUALLY, I THINK BLUNDERBOAR AND THE ANT PEOPLE ARE... ARE *ALLIES* OR SOMETHING, WORKING TOGETHER TO DESTROY COMPETITION UNDER THE GUISE OF URBAN WARFARE.

ANYTHING?
NOT THAT I COULD SEE.

BLUNDERBOAR MUST HAVE PEOPLE IN THE TRADE COMMISSION AND HAVE KNOWN ABOUT YOUR SHIPMENT. THE ANT PEOPLE PROBABLY ATTACKED THE IRON HORSE JUST TO STEAL YOUR SUPPLIES.

THOSE RAPSCALLIONS! THOSE VAGABONDS! WELL, THEIR GAME IS UP. I SHALL SIMPLY LOOK THOSE GIANTS IN THE EYE–

THEN YOU'D BETTER STAND ON A STOOL.

...*AHEM*,
AND DEMAND, OH UNSCRUPULOUS GIANTS, LET THIS CITY GO! YOU CLAIM ANT PEOPLE ARE THE REAL THREAT?
BALDERDASH!

YEAH, THAT'S A REAL SLICK PLAN FOR A FIRST TRY, BUT THERE MIGHT BE A HITCH OR TWO ON IMPLEMENTATION. IF–

SKREeeee
LOOK OUT!
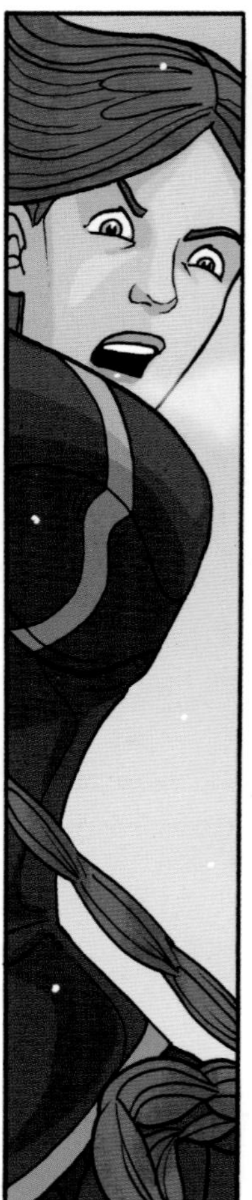

WHISH
YEE-HA!

SSSSSSSSS

TING
TING

KRUMP

LET'S HIGHTAIL IT, FOLKS. THOSE PEBBLES WON'T HOLD IT FOR LONG.

I SAY... AHEM... I, UH... HELLO, RAPUNZEL, WAS IT? I'M FREDDIE, AND YOU'RE... YOU'RE TALENTED, I SAY, AND QUITE THE CREATURE.

UH, THANKS,
UM, YOU'RE A NICE...
CREATURE, TOO.

ANT PEOPLE *AND* GIANTS?
THAT'LL BE ONE TOUGH TREASURE
HOUSE TO LIBERATE.

Did he touch her hand?

LOOK, I DON'T THINK IT'LL BE SAFE FOR YOU TO GO HOME, FREDDIE. BLUNDERBOAR MIGHT SEND ANT PEOPLE TO FINISH THE JOB. YOU HAVE A PLACE YOU CAN HIDE OUT?
INDEED. UH...
MY LADY, COULD I...WOULD YOU AND YOUR FRIENDS CARE TO ACCOMPANY ME TO... MY WORKSHOP IS A LITTLE RUSTIC...

BUT I COULD OFFER YOU SOME REFRESHMENT.
OR PING-PONG?
IT'S THE LATEST NOVELTY. WHEN THE BALLS BOUNCE, THEY MAKE THE MOST ENCHANTING POPPING SOUNDS.
MM-MM. NOTHING A PIXIE NEEDS LIKE A LITTLE REFRESHMENT, AND/OR PING-PONG.

I WOULDN'T MIND A CHANGE OF GARB AND A WASHUP. I FEEL HALF-BURIED AND MY HAIR'S FIT FOR A VERMIN'S NEST.
NONSENSE! THROUGH THE DUST OF VALOROUS ACTION, YOUR ENCHANTING EYES GLEAM ALL THE BRIGHTER.
GOLLY, THANKS, FREDDIE.
I'd had those very words on the tip of my tongue but loudmouth blurted first.
Actually, I'd been about to say, "You don't look that bad," which is basically the same thing.

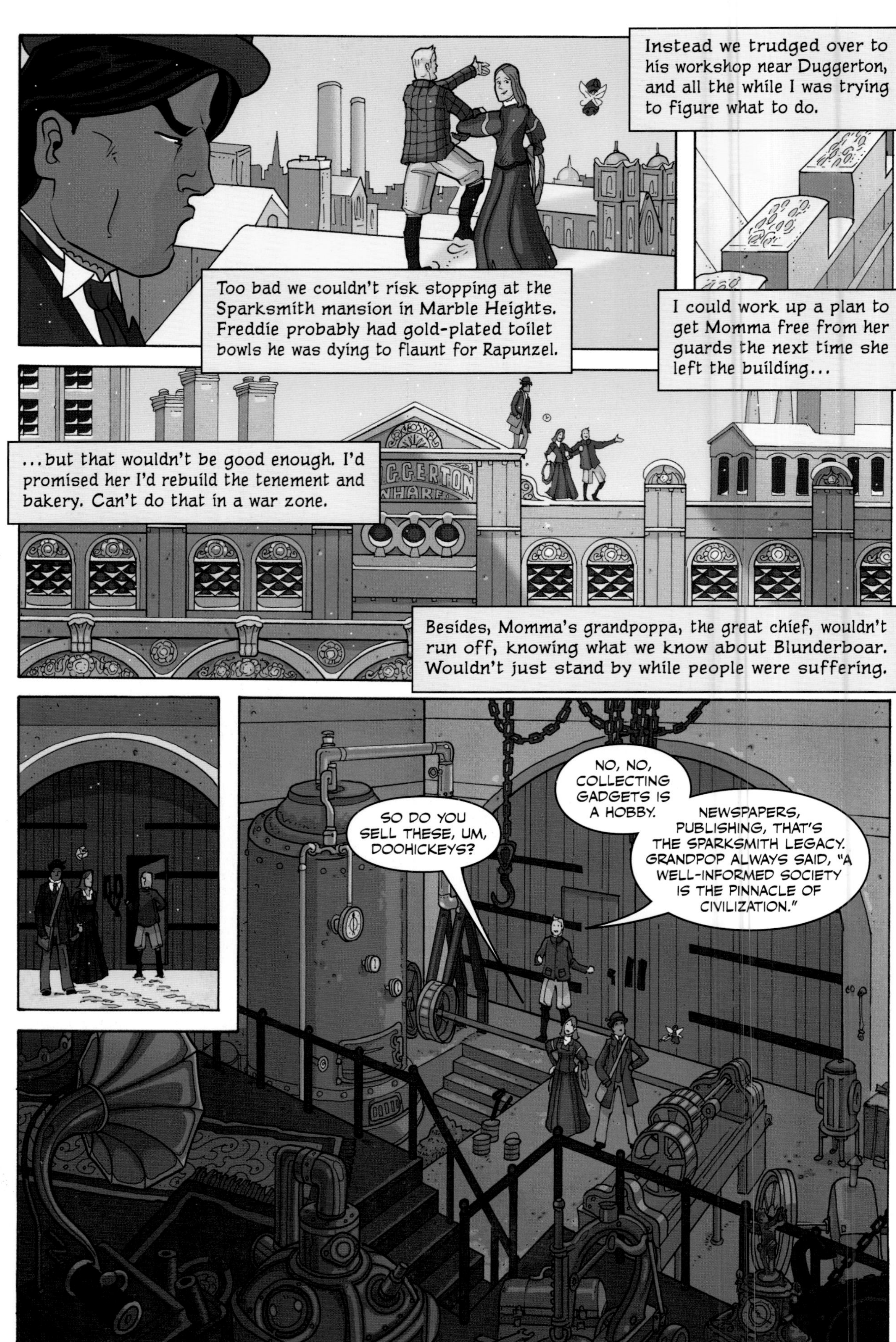
Instead we trudged over to his workshop near Duggerton, and all the while I was trying to figure what to do.
Too bad we couldn't risk stopping at the Sparksmith mansion in Marble Heights. Freddie probably had gold-plated toilet bowls he was dying to flaunt for Rapunzel.
I could work up a plan to get Momma free from her guards the next time she left the building...
...but that wouldn't be good enough. I'd promised her I'd rebuild the tenement and bakery. Can't do that in a war zone.
Besides, Momma's grandpoppa, the great chief, wouldn't run off, knowing what we know about Blunderboar. Wouldn't just stand by while people were suffering.
SO DO YOU SELL THESE, UM, DOOHICKEYS?
NO, NO, COLLECTING GADGETS IS A HOBBY.
NEWSPAPERS, PUBLISHING, THAT'S THE SPARKSMITH LEGACY. GRANDPOP ALWAYS SAID, "A WELL-INFORMED SOCIETY IS THE PINNACLE OF CIVILIZATION."

The current plan happened to consist solely of pretending I had a plan.

I'VE RECENTLY... OOF... MADE A MOST INGENIOUS PURCHASE... OUCH... FROM AN OVERSEAS CATALOG...
...THAT WILL SOLVE ALL OUR PROBLEMS!

BEHOLD THE BACKPACK-APULT.
STRAP IN, JACK, I SHALL SIMPLY FLING YOU AT YOUR LOFTY DESTINATION!
It was then I first suspected that Freddie wanted me dead.

UH, NO YOU WON'T. ANYTHING THAT GOES FLYING AT THAT THING RISKS BEING CAUGHT MIDAIR AND GNAWED TO A PULP BY A SKY-JEALOUS JABBERWOCK.

OR FALL SCREAMING TO HIS DEATH ON THE PAVEMENT BELOW...

BUT NICE THINKING, FREDDIE. WE'LL CALL THAT PLAN B.

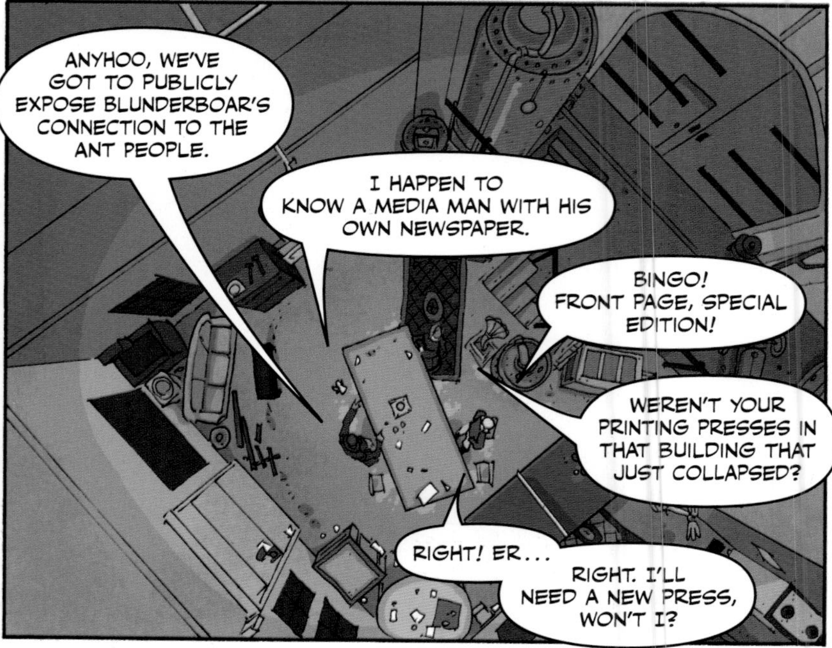
ANYHOO, WE'VE GOT TO PUBLICLY EXPOSE BLUNDERBOAR'S CONNECTION TO THE ANT PEOPLE.
I HAPPEN TO KNOW A MEDIA MAN WITH HIS OWN NEWSPAPER.
BINGO! FRONT PAGE, SPECIAL EDITION!
WEREN'T YOUR PRINTING PRESSES IN THAT BUILDING THAT JUST COLLAPSED?
RIGHT! ER...
RIGHT. I'LL NEED A NEW PRESS, WON'T I?

IT WON'T BE ENOUGH. THIS CITY'S IN LOVE WITH BLUNDERBOAR. WE NEED DEFINITE PROOF.

LIKE, SAY, AN ANT PERSON WILLING TO SPILL THE BEANS?

THAT'D DO.

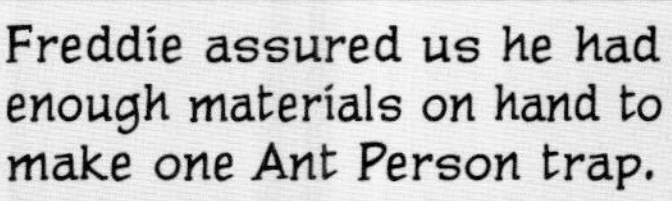
Freddie assured us he had enough materials on hand to make one Ant Person trap.

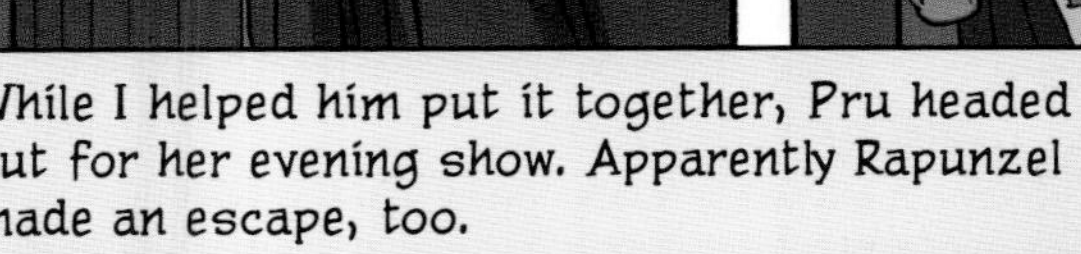
While I helped him put it together, Pru headed out for her evening show. Apparently Rapunzel made an escape, too.

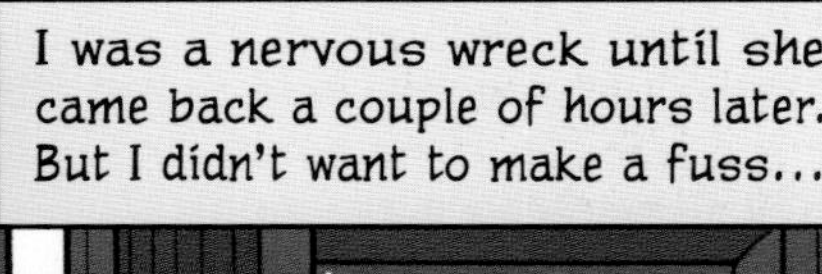
I was a nervous wreck until she came back a couple of hours later. But I didn't want to make a fuss...

...so I played it cool.
YOU JUST WENT OUT IN THE CITY? ALONE? BUT WHY? THIS ISN'T OUT WEST, PUNZIE. THE CITY IS DANGEROUS EVEN IF IT WEREN'T CURRENTLY A WAR ZONE.
YOU COULD'VE GOTTEN LOST OR KILLED OR BAKED INTO MUFFINS! WHAT WERE YOU DOING?

NOTHING, FORGET ABOUT IT.

Completely cool.

The next afternoon, we had something that might possibly hold an Ant Person for a minute. If we could find one and ask it nicely to step inside.
Brilliant plan, Jack.
I'LL NEED A FEW HOURS TO DO SOME RESEARCH.
RIGHT-O, CAPTAIN. WE'LL KEEP OURSELVES BUSY WHILE YOU DO THE BRAIN WORK.

MISS RAPUNZEL?
I...UH, I TOOK THE LIBERTY TO ORDER A CAKE. FOR YOU. BECAUSE YOU'RE, YOU KNOW, SWEET. LIKE CAKE. THAT IS, IF YOU'D LIKE SOME. CAKE.

REALLY?

JACK, DO YOU THINK I'M SWEET LIKE CAKE?

NOT ON YOUR LIFE.

OH.

'Cause she's not some silly pastry girl. She's strong and great and amazing and fun and beautiful and—

I LOVE CAKE!
BINGO!

I'D LIKE TO BINGO HIS—

JACKIE, JACKIE... ARE YOU TRYING TO LOSE HER?
WHAT? NO, I—

EE-GADS, BUCKO,
GIVE THAT GIRL A FLOWER OR YOU MIGHT BE SAYING TOODLES FOR GOOD.
COME ON, RAPUNZEL DOESN'T WANT A FLOWER.

IN ALL MY DIMINUTIVE YEARS, I'VE NEVER SEEN A GIRL WHO DIDN'T MELT AT GETTING A BLOOM FROM HER FELLA.

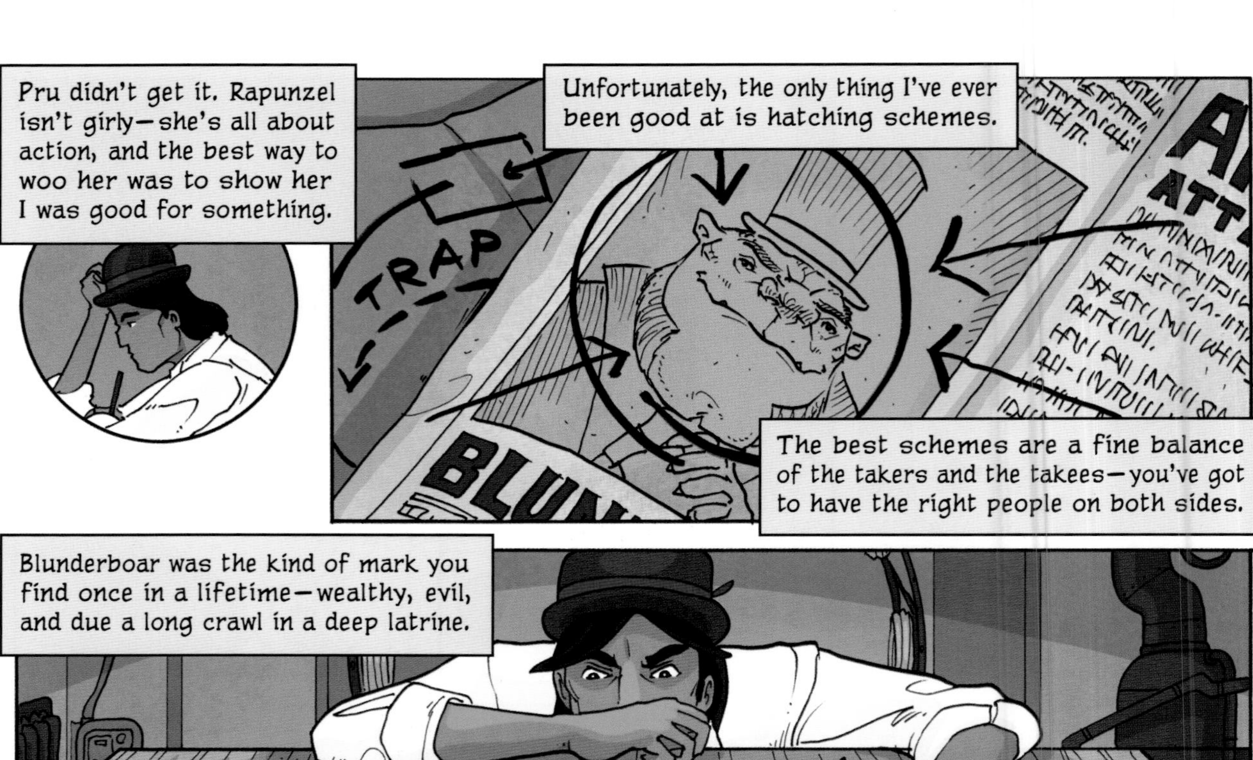
Pru didn't get it. Rapunzel isn't girly—she's all about action, and the best way to woo her was to show her I was good for something.
Unfortunately, the only thing I've ever been good at is hatching schemes.
TRAP
The best schemes are a fine balance of the takers and the takees—you've got to have the right people on both sides.

Blunderboar was the kind of mark you find once in a lifetime—wealthy, evil, and due a long crawl in a deep latrine.
But he had a fist the size of a boulder. If I tried to bring him down and failed, I was pretty sure there wouldn't be enough of me left to crawl anywhere.

But my mother had no one else. And Rapunzel expected me to succeed. It would be my greatest scheme ever or a fatal failure.
I perused Freddie's stash of newspapers from the past year...

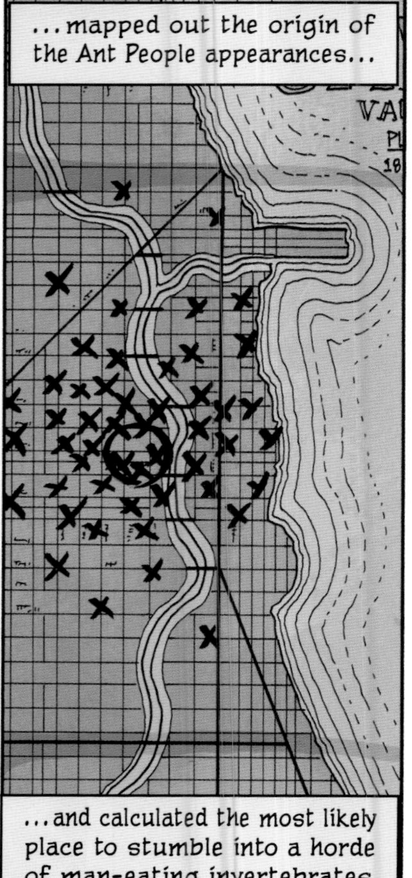
...mapped out the origin of the Ant People appearances...
...and calculated the most likely place to stumble into a horde of man-eating invertebrates.

The darkest, seediest, most unsavory quarter of Shyport...
Troll's Cranny.

If our luck held, we'd have the trap built before anyone tried to knife us.

But as is the case with my luck, it didn't hold.

OI! DIS 'ERE'S DA COMMODORE'S TURF, YE WEE WADDLEPUPPIES.
TONG TONG
I looked at that crook and wondered if that's how Rapunzel would see me, once she realized just what I am.

KRAK
BAD GUYS SURE ARE BAD, AREN'T THEY?
BAD IS BAD, THAT'S DARN TOOTIN'.
DID HE SAY "WADDLEPUPPY"?

CRUNCH

YOU'LL BE NEEDIN' TO PAY THE STRUTTIN' TOLL, SWEETAH CHEEKUMS.

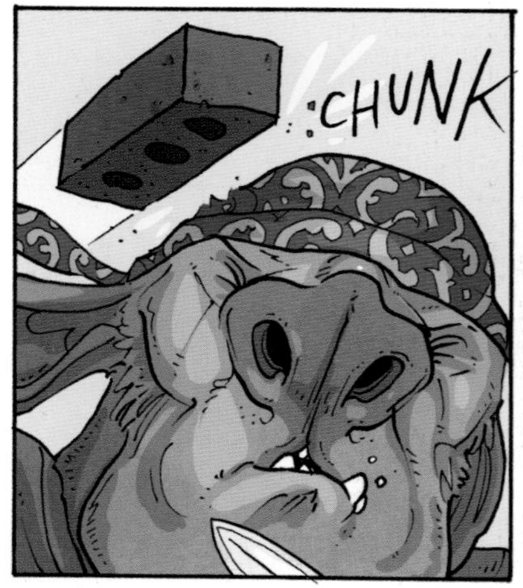
CHUNK

I MEAN, IT'S EASY TO TELL WHO THE BAD GUYS ARE.
SURE, THE ONES TRYING TO KILL US.

I was waiting for someone still bigger to show up and take care of this group for us...

...SWEETAH WHAT? WAS THAT AN INSULT?

NOT GETTING PAST US, YOU SPARE-RIBBED CONEY-HACKETS.

...but no such luck.

CONEY-HACKETS? SERIOUSLY. YOU'RE GOING WITH CONEY-HACKETS? YOU GUYS ARE RIDICULOUS.

FWISSSHH

YANK
Out West things were simpler—there's good and there's bad.

TOK
I wasn't sure Rapunzel would understand how in the city everything is a whole lot trickier.

FLIP

What would she do if she found out I used to be one of the bad guys?

CLONG

KRAK
SPANG
What if I still am?

HA-HA! I GUESS THOSE VILLAINS DIDN'T LIKE THE LOOK OF US.
OR THEY SAW SOMETHING WORSE...

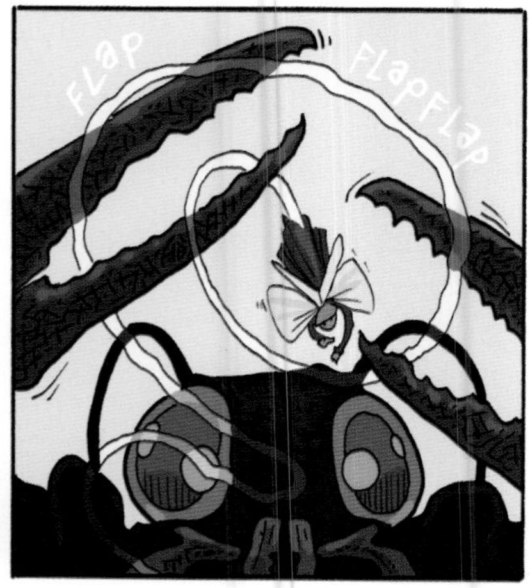

A follies gal at heart, Pru could do some fancy flying.

PUNZ, FRED, GET READY TO JUMP LEFT.
THESE FELLERS HERE SAID ANT PEOPLE WERE A BUNCH OF LILY-LIVERED . . . UM . . . BUM-SKEETERS!

UH-OH.

WHAM

SKREEEEEE

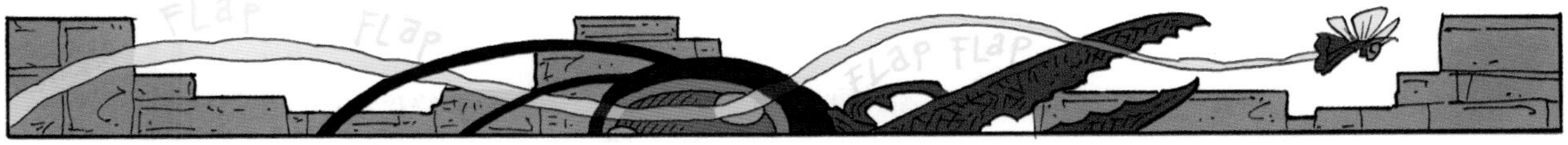
FLAP FLAP FLAP FLAP

THERE SHE IS. FREDDIE, PUNZIE, CIRCLE BACK.
AYE, CAPTAIN!
FLAP FLAP

FLAP FLAP FLAP

FLAP FLAP
SKREEEEEE

EEEE
CLICK

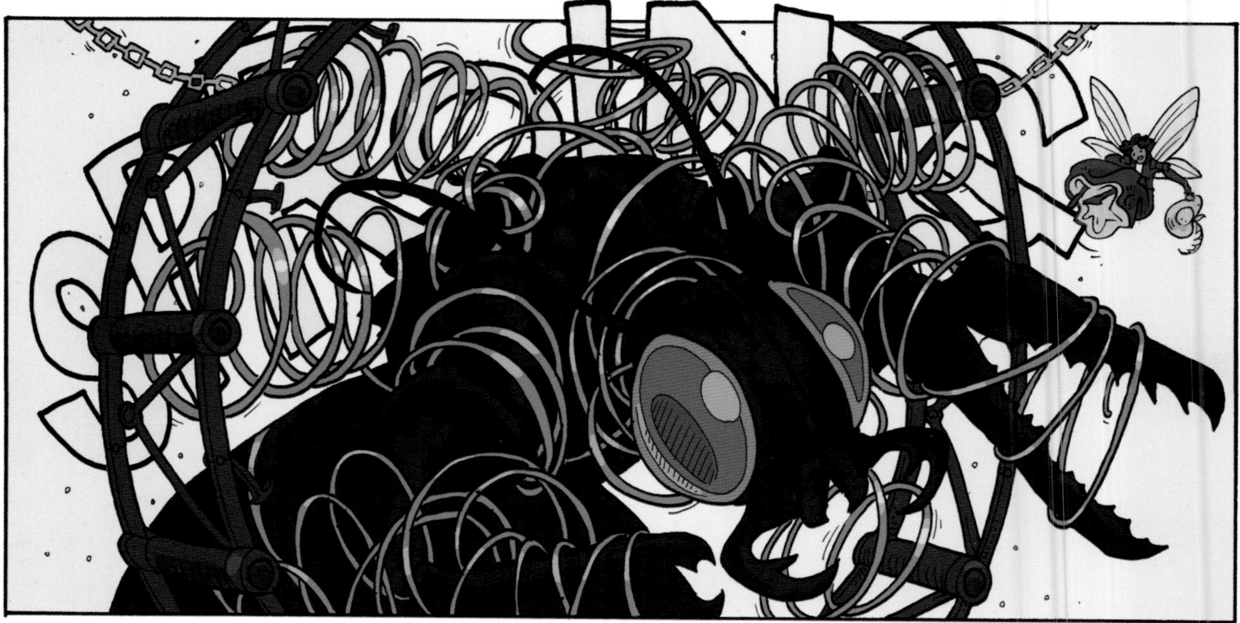

CLINK
CLINK

GOOD WORK.

TALK, YOU!
SKREE

WHAT...ER... WHAT EXACTLY ARE WE TRYING TO FIND OUT?
RIGHT...
WE'RE GOING TO NEED TO KNOW WHAT THE LARGER PLAN IS...

WHAT'S YOUR PLAN, FIEND?
TELL US!

FLIP FLIP FLIP

...WHAT IS IT THAT BLUNDERBOAR IS ORCHESTRATING THAT REQUIRES ANT PEOPLE?
SKREEEE

WHAT IS BLUNDERBOAR UP TO, DEMONSPAWN?
WHY WOULD ANT PEOPLE EVEN WORK WITH A GIANT?
WHAT IS HE OFFERING THEM?

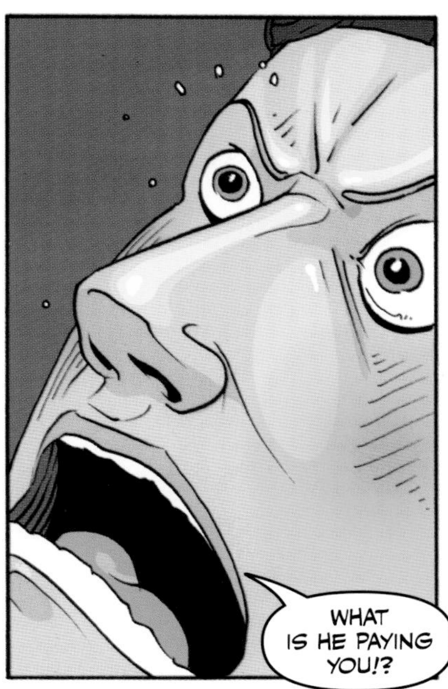
WHAT IS HE PAYING YOU!?

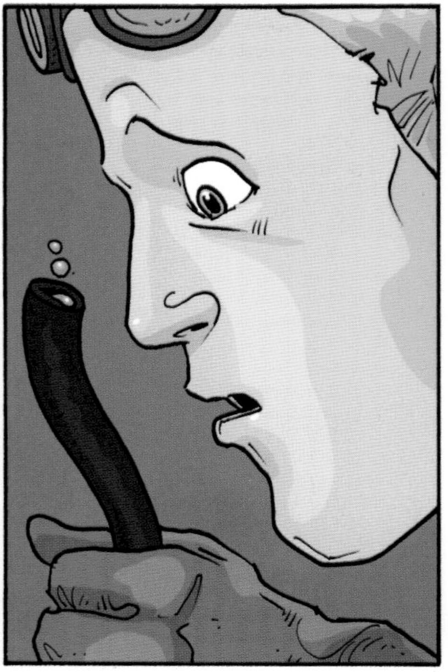

We needed to talk to whoever was leading the ants. And get them to turn on Blunderboar.
WHERE IS YOUR LEADER?
SKREE.
WHAT?
SKREE.
ALL WE SEEM TO BE GETTING IS A LOT OF *SKREE*.
I WAS NOTICING THAT MYSELF.

IT DOESN'T MAKE ANY SENSE. THEY HAVE TO BE ABLE TO COMMUNICATE, OR NONE OF THIS WOULD GET ORGANIZED!

TAKE A LOOK AT THIS, CAPTAIN.
JUST JACK IS FINE. WHAT IS IT?

A CLUE... SHROUDED IN MYSTERY BY ARCANE ORIENTISH PAPER-CREASING!
JUST UNFOLD IT, FREDDIE.
OH.

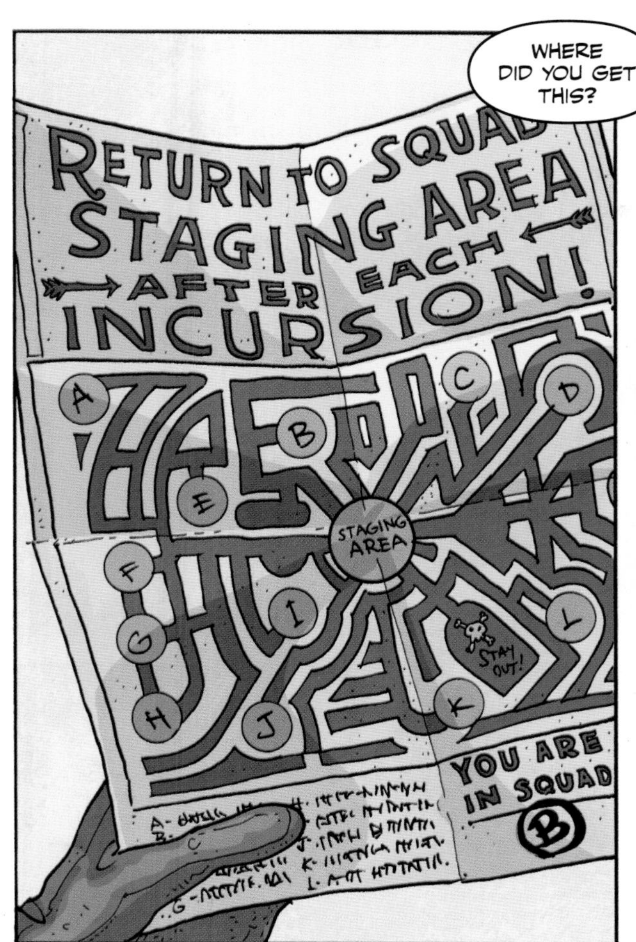
RETURN TO SQUAD STAGING AREA AFTER EACH INCURSION!
STAGING AREA
STAY OUT!
YOU ARE IN SQUAD B

WHERE DID YOU GET THIS?
I PULLED IT OUT OF... ITS... UM... REAR...
OUT OF ITS REAR END? EW!

NO, NO, NO. ITS REAR... CARAPACE. IT WAS JUST STICKING OUT.
WHATEVER. EW.

THIS IS WHERE THEY ARE. WHERE ALL OF THEM ARE.
SO NOW WE KNOW WHERE NOT TO GO.
I'M GOING DOWN THERE.
WHY? YOU THINK THERE'S TREASURE?
NO, I THINK THERE'S LEVERAGE. IF WE CAN FIND OUT WHAT BLUNDERBOAR DOESN'T WANT ANYONE TO KNOW, WE'VE GOT THE UPPER HAND. BETTER YET, IF WE CAN STEER THINGS IN A DIRECTION HE ISN'T EXPECTING...

IT GOES WITHOUT SAYING THAT I'LL BE GOING WITH YOU.
LOOK, THIS IS GOING TO REQUIRE SOME SERIOUS FAST-TALKING, AND YOU'LL–

TELL ME YOU'RE NOT WORRIED ABOUT MY SAFETY. YOU DO REMEMBER THE GIANT SNAKE?
IT'S JUST, I'M HOPING TO DO THIS WITHOUT A FIGHT, AND MY... TRICK WILL BE MORE BELIEVABLE IF I'M ALONE.

HMPH.
RIGHT. HMPH.

OKAY. I'LL NEED A... A REAR GUARD.
THAT WAY YOU'LL BE READY TO COME RUNNING IF I NEED HELP.

BUT DON'T COME UNLESS I HOLLER. NO NEED FOR ALL OF US TO LOSE OUR LIVERS.
FINE.

BUT YOU BETTER BE CAREFUL, JACK THE BAKER'S SON.

DON'T WORRY ABOUT ME.
I'M WILY.
Also, fairly stupid.
But only on occasion.

Such as when I'm descending alone into a sewer hive of gargantuan flesh-eating insect people.
Right about when that dank, rotten stench hit me I questioned the whole going-it-alone thing.

But it was the kind of deed that'd make my momma proud, wasn't it?
The sort of thing good guys did?

The type of heroic action that Rapunzel could admire.

HELLO?
UM...
ANT PEOPLE?
SKREE?

I'M UNARMED. I'M A... FRIEND. NO NEED FOR BITING OR TEARING OR EATING...

JUST CAME TO TALK.
BLUNDERBOAR SENT ME.

SKREE?
AAH!

OH...GOOD. HERE YOU ARE. JUST AS I...JUST AS BLUNDERBOAR SAID. LISTEN, THERE'S BEEN A CHANGE OF PLANS.
WHAT?
RIGHT. YOU DO SPEAK—*AHEM.* SO, THIS EVENING AT EXACTLY FIVE, BLUNDERBOAR WANTS YOU TO POP UP ON FLEET STREET IN FRONT OF THE *SHYPORT LEDGER* BUILDING, SHOUT "*SKREE*" A LOT, THE USUAL. EXCEPT NO KILLING THIS TIME. WHAT A DRAG, HUH?

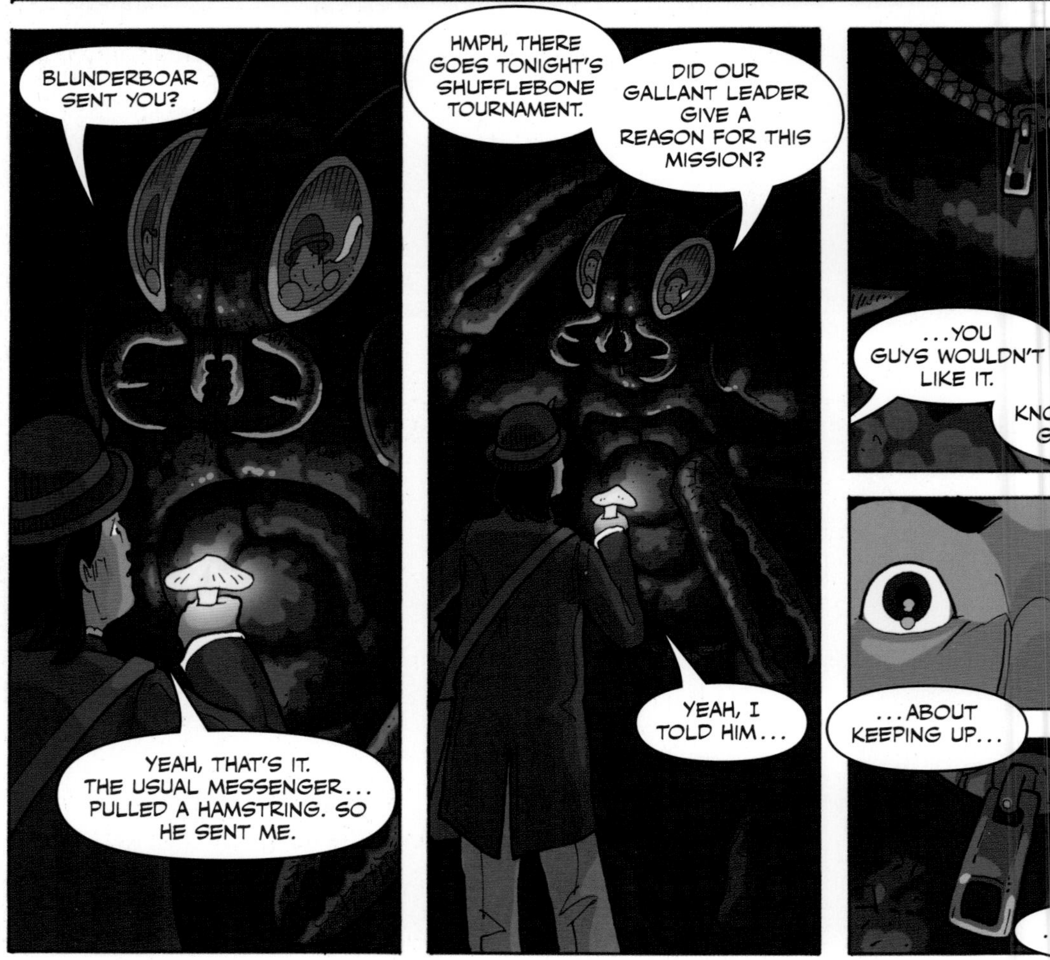
BLUNDERBOAR SENT YOU?
YEAH, THAT'S IT. THE USUAL MESSENGER... PULLED A HAMSTRING. SO HE SENT ME.
HMPH, THERE GOES TONIGHT'S SHUFFLEBONE TOURNAMENT.
DID OUR GALLANT LEADER GIVE A REASON FOR THIS MISSION?
YEAH, I TOLD HIM...
...YOU GUYS WOULDN'T LIKE IT.
BUT YOU KNOW HOW THOSE GIANTS ARE...
...ABOUT KEEPING UP...
...APPEARANCES.

UM... OF COURSE YOU WOULD KNOW, BECAUSE YOU *ARE* GIANTS. UNDER THERE.
WHICH IS A THING I'VE KNOWN ALL ALONG.

RIGHT.

EXACTLY.

SO... SHUFFLEBONE? ANYONE?
EAT HIM.
SPLORT
AAH!

AAH! HOLY GRAVY! GREAT CRACKLIN' CORNBREAD!

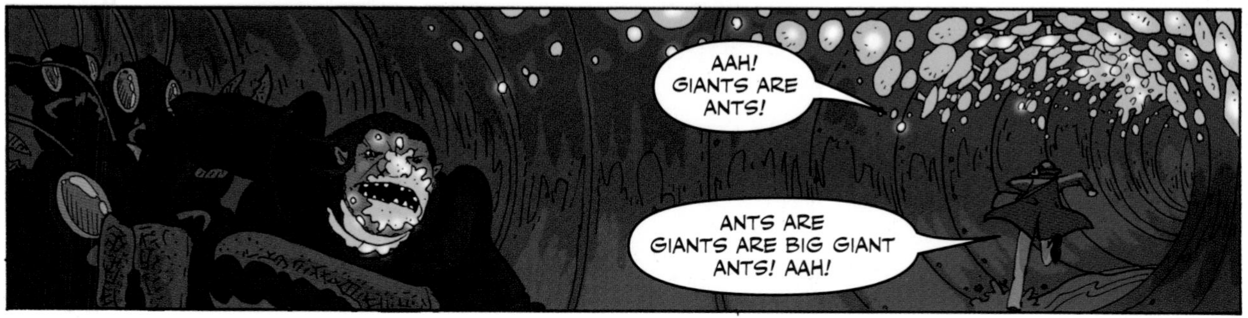
AAH! GIANTS ARE ANTS!
ANTS ARE GIANTS ARE BIG GIANT ANTS! AAH!

Sorry, Momma. I didn't want you to be right about me, but you were. Sorry.

COO COO

WHAT WAS THAT?
WHAT?

THAT IMPOSSIBLY LOUD, DEAFENING *COO*.
OH THAT. I THOUGHT YOU MEANT SOMETHING ELSE.

WHAT THE . . .
THEY HAVE MAGICKED BIRD BEASTIES!

AAH!
HELP!

Three giant pigeons living in the sewer.
ATTACK! ATTACK!
Three magic beans I tossed at some birds near a sewer grate last year.

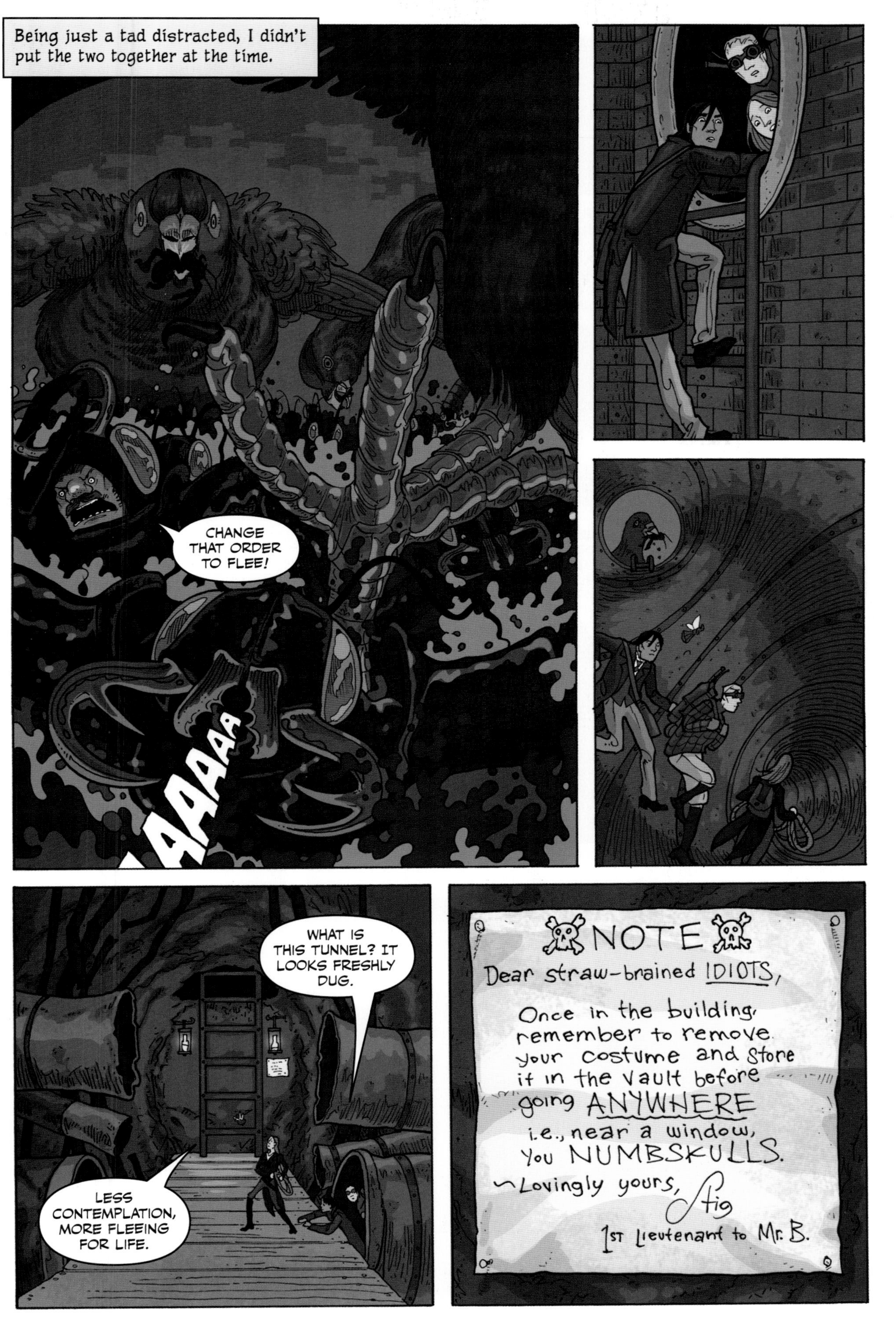

Being just a tad distracted, I didn't put the two together at the time.

CHANGE THAT ORDER TO FLEE!

AAAAAA

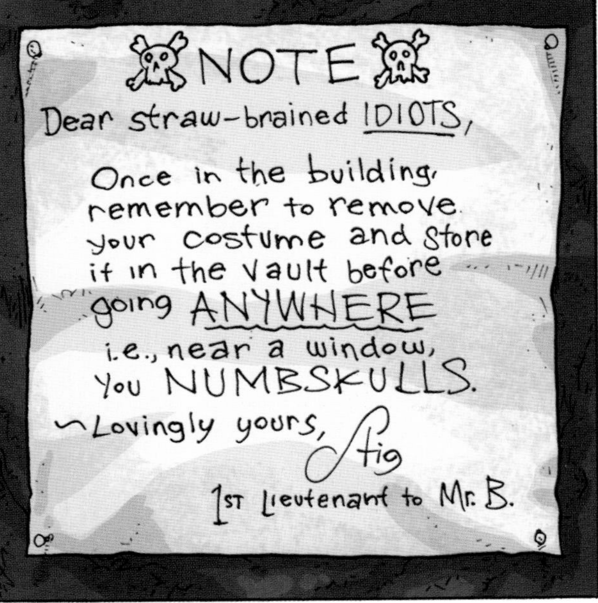

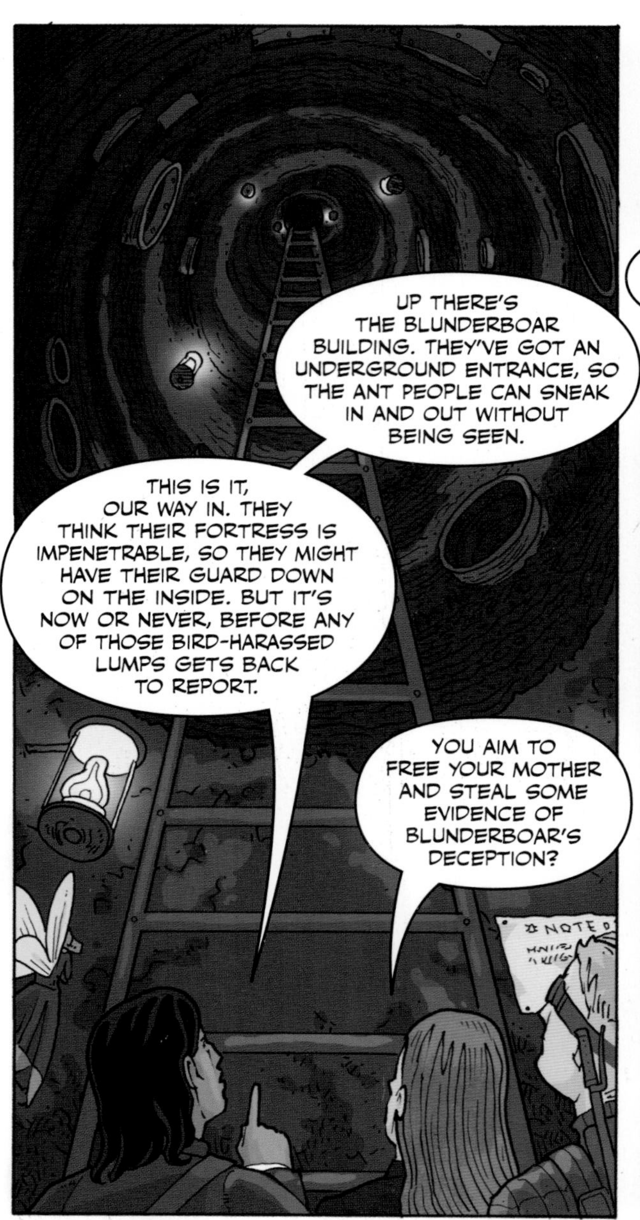
UP THERE'S THE BLUNDERBOAR BUILDING. THEY'VE GOT AN UNDERGROUND ENTRANCE, SO THE ANT PEOPLE CAN SNEAK IN AND OUT WITHOUT BEING SEEN.
THIS IS IT, OUR WAY IN. THEY THINK THEIR FORTRESS IS IMPENETRABLE, SO THEY MIGHT HAVE THEIR GUARD DOWN ON THE INSIDE. BUT IT'S NOW OR NEVER, BEFORE ANY OF THOSE BIRD-HARASSED LUMPS GETS BACK TO REPORT.
YOU AIM TO FREE YOUR MOTHER AND STEAL SOME EVIDENCE OF BLUNDERBOAR'S DECEPTION?

WHAT ABOUT OUR TRAPPED ANT PERSON?
TROLL'S CRANNY IS TEEMING WITH ANT PEOPLE. OURS IS SURELY FREED BY NOW. SO . . . WE'LL HAVE TO GO THROUGH THE BUILDING UP TO THE ROOF, AND THEN CLIMB INTO THAT FLOATING STORY.
THERE MIGHT STILL BE ANT PEOPLE COSTUMES IN A CLOSET NEAR BLUNDERBOAR'S STATEROOM. THAT MIGHT JUST CONVINCE THE MAYOR AND ALL OF SHYPORT.

HOW DO YOU KNOW WHERE THE COSTUMES WOULD BE?
I'M PRETTY SURE I SAW SOME THE TIME I CLIMBED THE BEANSTALK.

YOU MEAN, YOU'VE ACTUALLY BEEN INSIDE THAT PLACE?
YEAH, JUST FOR A MINUTE.
Most terrifying minute of my short life.

BUT I THOUGHT THE BEANSTALK FELL DOWN AND . . . AND I DIDN'T KNOW YOU ACTUALLY GOT UP THERE. WHY DIDN'T YOU TELL ME?
'CAUSE I HAD TO SKIP TOWN FAST. AND WE BETTER SKIP THIS SEWER BEFORE WE'RE FOUND.

I sent Prudence off to find my mother in Blunderboar's kitchen, warn her what we were up to...
...and get Momma out of the building if she could, or at least find a good hiding place, in case we got caught.

ROLF, WHERE DID YOU PUT THE BUBBLE BATH?
HEY, WHO–

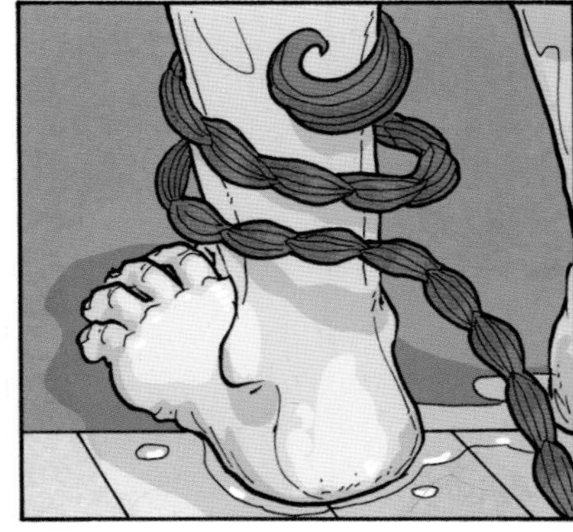

YEE-HA!

UH!
SLIP

SMACK

LET OFF, YOU GNATS!

UGH.
OW!

OOF!

THAT WAS...
TOUGH.
YEAH.
AAAAAAAAAAAA

FREDDIE, YOU HAVE ANY MORE OF THAT ANT-TRAP WIRE?
WHAM
WHAT? OH? YES, RIGHT-O!

GROOOOAAAAN

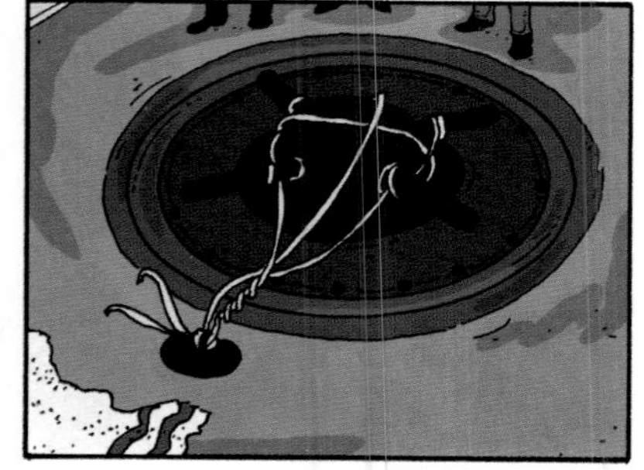

THIS VERTI-LIFT TAKES A KEY TO OPERATE, AND I DIDN'T SEE STAIRS.

THEN I GUESS IT'S MY TURN.

HELP?

Oh, all right, fine...

DING

...AND THAT'S WHEN I ADD A HANDFUL OF MINCED GARLIC.

AND IT DOESN'T OVERWHELM THE FLAVOR?

WELL, YOU SEE, OFFSET BY THE LEMON JUICE...

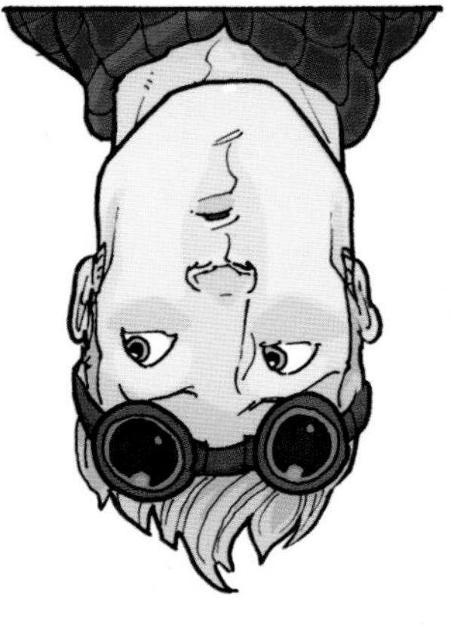

PUNZIE?
YEAH?
Do I tell her she's pretty, that my heart goes *bang* every time she hog-ties a giant, that I have to look away for fear of drowning in her eyes? That I don't want to be a criminal mastermind anymore?

YOU—
YOU'RE GOOD AT LASSOING STUFF.
THANKS...
Ah, the words that flow from my mouth are pure poetry....

WHEN WE REACH THE TOP FLOOR, FIND STAIRS TO THE ROOF AND WE'RE NEARLY HOME FREE.

DING

FEE. FI. FO, AND, OH LET'S SAY, FUM.

AND YOU SAY, PRUDENCE DEAR, THAT THIS ISN'T THE FIRST TIME HE'S LEFT YOU BEHIND AS HE BREAKS INTO MY HOME? BAD FORM.
HIYA, JACKIE.
Ain't that just daisy.

Part 4: The Blunderboar Job

TWACK

YOUNG LADY, DON'T TRIFLE WITH ME.

THE GAME IS OVER.

BUT IS IT? HA-HA!

CHWANG

RATS.
I'M SORRY, MOMMA.

APOLOGIES, JACK, BUT I'VE GOT A NEW PARTNER, AND HE PAID ME A TIDY BUNDLE TO TURN YOU OVER. YOU KNOW HOW IT IS.

NO, PRUDENCE,

ACTUALLY I DON'T.

MAUDE, THIS PIXIE HAS PAINTED A VERY INTERESTING STORY OF A BOY WHO PLANS BIG SCHEMES TO GET GAIN, NO MATTER WHOM HE HURTS. WHAT A TRIAL HE MUST HAVE BEEN. MY OWN DEAR MOTHER OFTEN DEPLORED HAVING TO RAISE A SCHEMING GENIUS SON.

I'M NOT LIKE YOU.

YOU BREAK INTO MY HOME...
...STEAL MY GOOSE...

...AND IN THE PROCESS DESTROY A BUILDING AND COMMIT NEGLIGENT GIGANTICIDE.

CLUMSY? YES. PATHETIC? OBVIOUSLY.
BUT GIVE YOU SOME MUSCLE TO BACK YOU UP, REFINE YOUR SENSE OF STYLE AND SHOWMANSHIP...

...AND MY BOY, YOU *ARE* ME.

IMITATION IS PURE FLATTERY, BUT YOU MAY HAVE GUESSED, I'M NOT FOND OF COMPETITION.

UH, MR. B? I KNOW I SUGGESTED RIPPING SOME LIMBS FROM VARIOUS LIMBS, BUT NOW I'M THINKING, HOW'S ABOUT A GOOD SCOLDING AND SENDING HIM ON HIS WAY?

SHE'S SERVED HER PURPOSE. SOMEBODY STUFF HER IN A BOX.
WHAT?!

HOW DARE YOU, YOU WALKING MUDSLIDE?

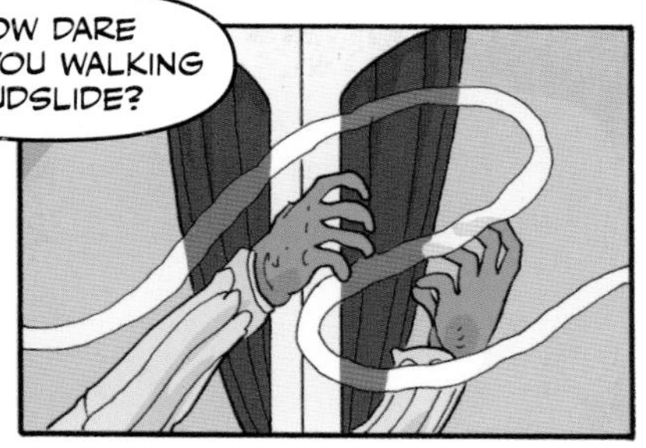

JACK, WHAT'S THE PLAN?
PLAN? NO PLAN. IT'S DEAD. I FAILED. THE END.

GET HER!

COME ON, YOU ALWAYS HAVE A PLAN B–
AND THAT PLAN WILL BLOW UP, TOO. I ALWAYS FAIL. RAPUNZEL, IT'S TIME YOU KNEW–I'VE BEEN PRETENDING TO BE THE KIND OF FELLA YOU MIGHT LIKE.
BUT BLUNDERBOAR'S RIGHT ABOUT ME–I'M . . . I'M JUST A LOW-DOWN CRIMINAL WITH A CHRONIC CASE OF BAD LUCK, AND IF YOU WANT NOTHING TO DO WITH ME, I'LL UNDERSTAND.
HOLD STILL, YOU SLIPPERY PIXIE!
OW! SHE BIT ME!

WELL, NO WONDER THINGS DON'T WORK OUT WHEN YOU'VE GOT IT INTO YOUR FAT HEAD TO PLAY AT SOMETHING YOU'RE NOT.

"I'M A NO-GOOD CRIMINAL, BLUNDERBOAR'S RIGHT..." NICE TRY, BUT I CAN TELL CLEAR AS WATER THAT YOU JUST DON'T HAVE THE BONES FOR IT.

CRRAACK

...SO TO SPEAK.
LISTEN, I'M SORRY. I WANTED TO BE SOMEONE...SOMEONE LIKE YOU, BUT THE TRUTH IS I'M–

DON'T MAKE ME SMACK YOU, JACK. I'M NOT STUPID, I'VE ALWAYS KNOWN EXACTLY WHAT YOU ARE.
YOU MAY HAVE A TOUCH OF BAD LUCK AND A FEW UNFORTUNATE HABITS, BUT YOU'RE ONE OF THE GOOD GUYS, NO DOUBT ABOUT IT.

YOU ACTUALLY THINK–
'COURSE I DO.

IT'S WHY I LOVE YOU.
YOU...
...OH.

BUT IF THE GOOD GUYS ARE GOING TO WIN, WE NEED THE PLAN, JACK. SO COME ON, LET'S GO MAKE IT HAPPEN.
Make it happen. Make it happen.

A perfect scheme really is all about having the right mark...

...and the right team.

For the first time in my life, everything was exactly right.
So, Plan B...

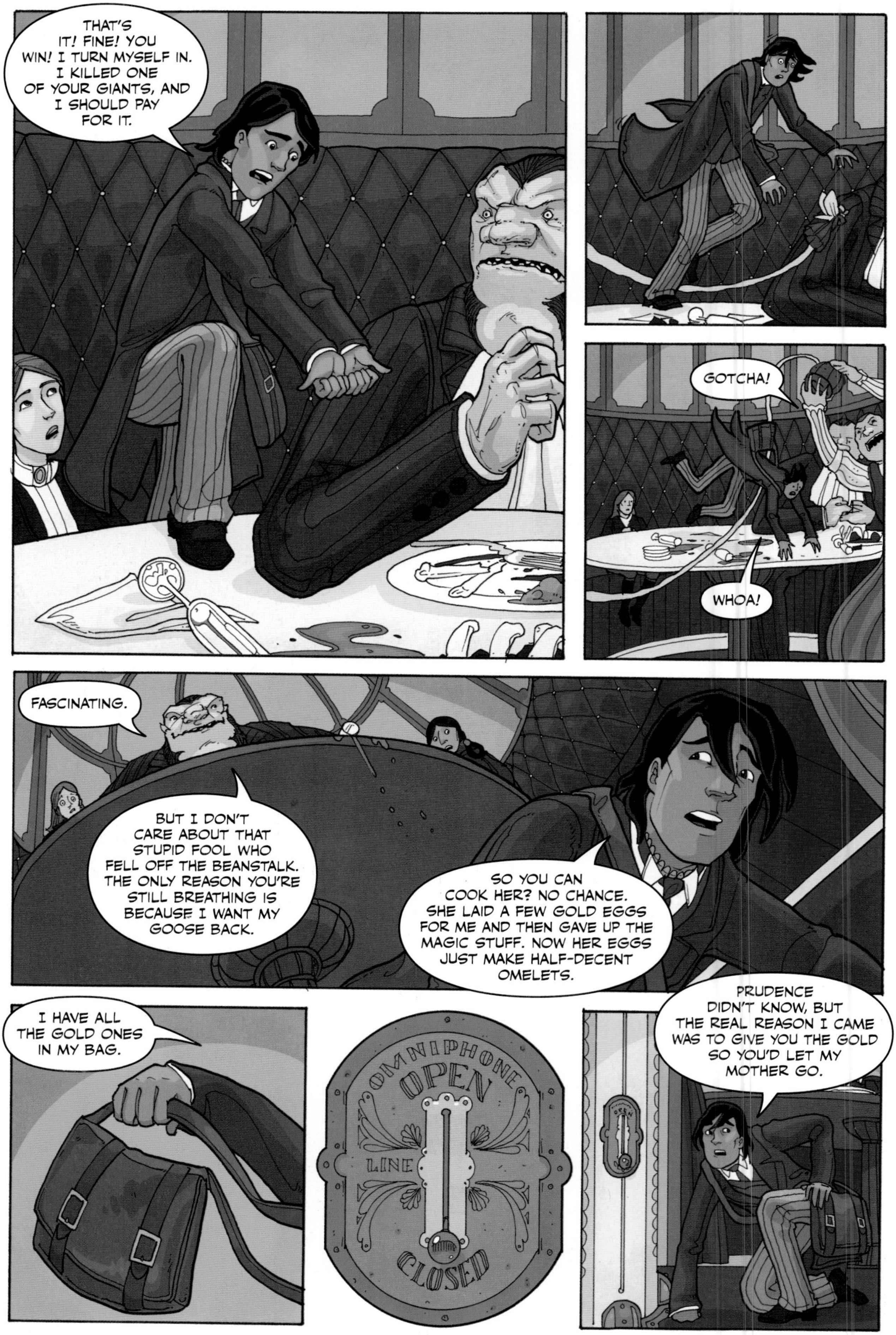

FASCINATING.

BUT I DON'T CARE ABOUT THAT STUPID FOOL WHO FELL OFF THE BEANSTALK. THE ONLY REASON YOU'RE STILL BREATHING IS BECAUSE I WANT MY GOOSE BACK.

SO YOU CAN COOK HER? NO CHANCE. SHE LAID A FEW GOLD EGGS FOR ME AND THEN GAVE UP THE MAGIC STUFF. NOW HER EGGS JUST MAKE HALF-DECENT OMELETS.

I HAVE ALL THE GOLD ONES IN MY BAG.

OMNIPHONE
OPEN
LINE
CLOSED

PRUDENCE DIDN'T KNOW, BUT THE REAL REASON I CAME WAS TO GIVE YOU THE GOLD SO YOU'D LET MY MOTHER GO.

CLICK
THEY'RE YOURS, BLUNDERBOAR, SO LONG AS YOU AGREE TO GIVE MY MOTHER THIS BUILDING AFTER SHYPORT TURNS YOU OUT.

OH BY ALL MEANS! I AGREE! THE VERY MOMENT I'M RUN OFF!
FEH!
YOU REALLY ARE A FOOL, AND YOUR WINGED FRIEND NEARLY HAD ME CONVINCED THAT YOU WERE CLEVER.

AH, IT'S JUST AS WELL. THE STUPID GO DOWN THE GULLET MUCH EASIER.
ARE YOU GOING TO KILL ME NOW, BLUNDERBOAR?
GRIND MY BONES INTO BREAD AND ALL THAT?

A DIET OF HUMAN BONES DOES WORK WONDERS FOR A GIANT'S STRENGTH, THAT'S TRUE, BUT SIMPLY KILL YOU? NO. I'M THINKING I'LL GNAW YOU TO DEATH FIRST, LIKE WE USED TO DO IN THE OLD WORLD.

I'M NOT IMMUNE TO NOSTALGIA.

SO ALL THIS ANT PEOPLE STUFF STARTED TO COVER UP YOUR MURDERS? YOU AND YOUR LOT HAVE JUST BEEN KILLING PEOPLE FOR THEIR BONES.
HMM, HOW SMALL-MINDED OF YOU.
THE BONES WERE SIMPLY AN ADDED BONUS. FIRST AND FOREMOST, I AM A BUSINESSMAN.

KEEP SIDESTEPPING, BAKER'S SON. I ENJOY PRE-DINNER CALISTHENICS.
THEN DRESSING UP IN SILLY ANT COSTUMES WHEN YOU ATTACKED YOUR COMPETITION WAS A WAY TO PUT THEM OUT OF THE MARKET WITHOUT BEING CAUGHT. A LITTLE SHOWY, WASN'T IT?
THE MASSES PREFER THEIR TRAGEDIES TO BE ENTERTAINING.
THEN WHEN PANIC ENSUED, YOU KINDLY LENT BLUNDERBOAR CORPS TO THE MAYOR TO TAKE CARE OF THE IMAGINARY PROBLEM. AND SUDDENLY, YOU'RE IN CHARGE OF THE CITY.
YOU ARE CLEVER AFTER ALL. PITY. I MAY NEED EXTRA BUTTER TO CHOKE YOU DOWN.
DO YOU KNOW WHAT YOUR IDIOT PLAN HAS DONE TO THIS CITY? WHEN THEY FIND OUT THAT YOU'RE NO HERO, THEY'LL MAKE YOU PAY.
THE POLICE FORCE IS PURE BUFFOONERY. EVEN IF THE PATHETIC PEOPLE OF THIS WRETCHED CITY OPENED THEIR EYES, WHAT COULD THEY DO AGAINST ME? THROW ROCKS?

eee
IF THAT'S WHAT–
THAT CURSED BROWNIE SCREAM. WHAT SET THEM OFF?
eeeeet

eeeeeeeeee
IT'S A MOB OF PEOPLE. THEY'RE . . . UH . . . THEY'RE THROWING ROCKS.

DON'T RUN AWAY FROM A LITTLE SCREAM! THAT'S MY NEPHEW JACKIE UP THERE TELLING BLUNDERBOAR WHAT'S WHAT. KEEP THOSE ROCKS COMING!

DON'T REEL IN THE BROWNIES YET. WE NEED TO KEEP THAT MOB BACK.

BUT WHY ARE THEY–
OOH, I MIGHT HAVE ACCIDENTALLY TURNED ON YOUR LITTLE MACHINE HERE.
IT LOOKS LIKE THE WHOLE "WRETCHED CITY" HEARD YOUR "PATHETIC PEOPLE" SPEECH.

eeeeee
HA-HA! THAT'LL DO IT!

GRRRRRRRRRRRRRRRRRR

ARGH!
DON'T TOUCH HIM! DON'T TOUCH MY BOY!
eeeeeeeeeee

LET ME OUT. I CAN STOP THOSE BROWNIES SO THE MOB CAN GET PAST.
FAT CHANCE.

PLEASE! I MADE A MISTAKE. I WANT TO SEE BLUNDERBOAR SQUIRM.

YOU'VE GOT TEN SECONDS, SPARKLES. MESS UP AGAIN, AND I FEED YOU TO A CAT.

KRASH

EEEEEEEEEEEEEEEEEE

EEEEEEEEEE
CRASH
PIXIE SISTERS, GIVE THOSE BROWNIES SOMETHING TO SCREAM ABOUT!

IS THAT PRUDENCE UP THERE?
EEEEE

UHHH...
EEEEE

THEY GOT PRUDENCE!
COME ON, GIRLS!
EEEEE

EEEEEE

GET 'EM!

HOW ARE YA?
LIVE AROUND HERE?
HI THERE.
HI.
HELLO.
HI.

UH, HEY THERE.
HI.
THAT SURE IS A PRETTY HAT.
BRISK OUT, ISN'T IT?
GEE, I'D SURE LIKE TO GET RID OF THIS ANKLE CHAIN.
I KNOW A DUGGER WITH SOME METAL CUTTERS...

YES!
HOORAY!

BLUNDERBOR
GET 'EM!

LET'S GET OUT OF HERE!
KRASH

YOU COULD STICK AROUND TO KILL US, OR YOU COULD ESCAPE.

AARGH! YOU LITTLE RODENT. I'LL SQUASH–
HURRY, BOSS, BEFORE THAT MOB GETS UP HERE.

JACK, MY BOY, THERE'S SOMETHING I SHOULD'VE TOLD YOU LONG AGO.

YES?

YOU'RE COMING WITH ME. PLENTY OF BONES TO GRIND IN THE OLD WORLD.

NO!

LET HER GO!

ROOF ACCESS
THEY'RE GETTING AWAY!

CLATCH
SNIK
SNIK

NO YOU DON'T...

RAPUNZEL!

LEWIS, ATTACK!

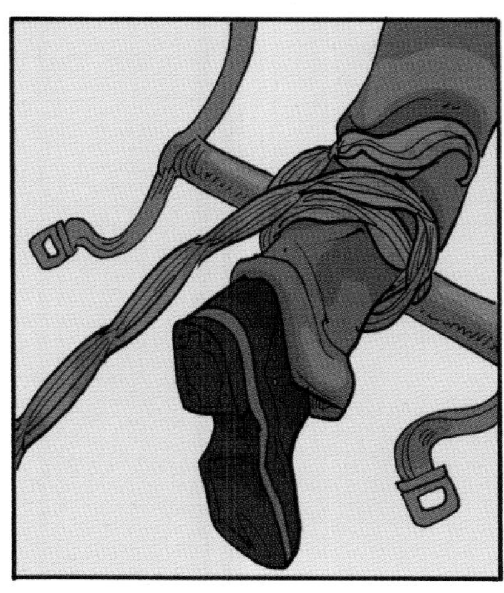

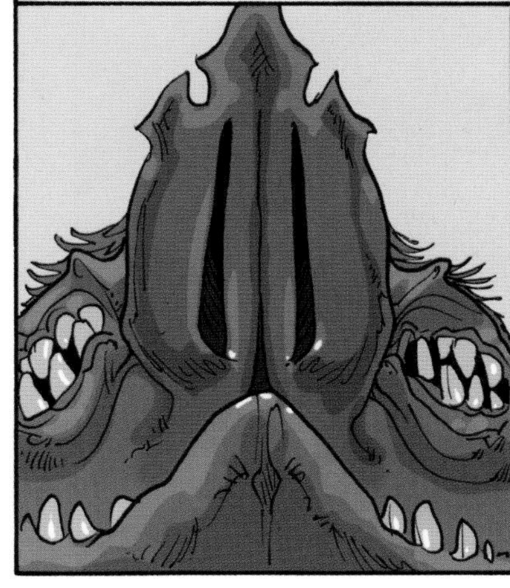

SHLORP

SSSSSSS
SSSSSSS

GET OFF!
AAAH!
SNRG.

SNRG!

SNRG?

SPIT
SPLURT
SPIT

SSSS
SSSSSS
SPLAT
SSSSSS

AAAAAAAAAAAAAAAAAA

THUD

WE GOTTA...
WE GOTTA...

FREDDIE, TELL ME YOU'RE WEARING IT. TELL ME YOU BROUGHT THAT STUPID CATAPULT BACKPACK.

BINGO! STRAP ON, VALIANT LEADER.

OH BOY.

LISTEN... THANKS.
GO SAVE YOUR LADY, MY HEROIC FRIEND. SHE IS WORTH KEEPING, I'D SAY.

YOU GOT THAT RIGHT.

I . . . CAN'T REACH . . . THE LEVER . . .
THE CATCH IS STUCK!
HI . . . UM,
COULD A PENITENT PIXIE WITH A MILD CONCUSSION LEND A HAND?

AU REVOIR.
LADDER RELEASE
CLICK

SNIK
SNIK

EEE!

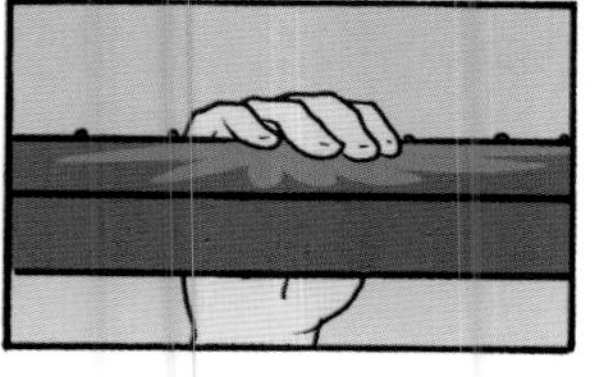

AAAAAAA!

Yep.
My best plan ever.
NO-NO-NO-NO...
I'm a genius.
OOMPH.
OKAY, OKAY, I'M NOT DEAD.
YET.
SHIFTING TO FLIGHT MODE...
CHANK
YAH.
THIS IS JUST DAISY.

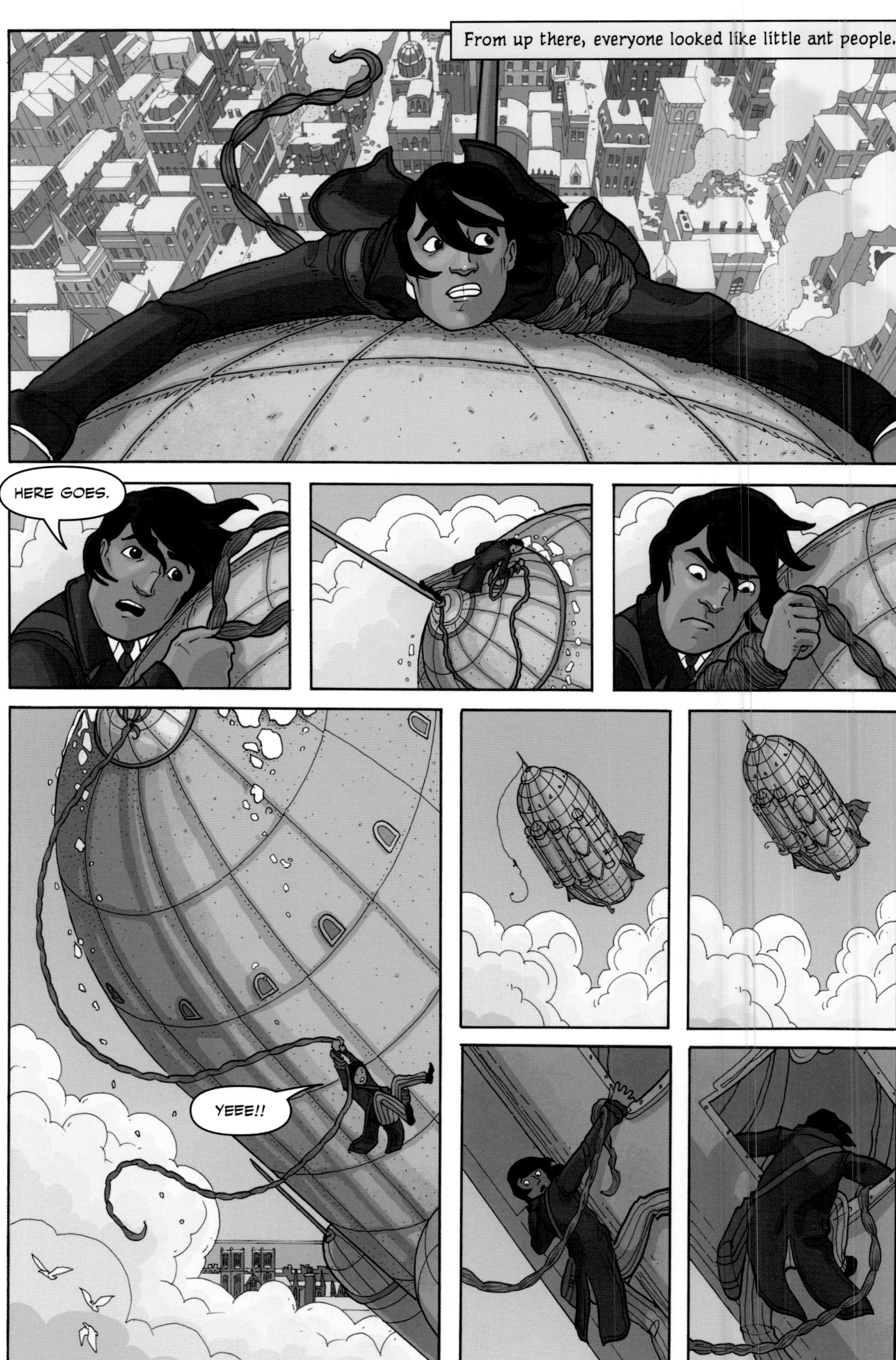
From up there, everyone looked like little ant people.
HERE GOES.
YEEE!!

MOMMA! YOU'RE OKAY!

YOU CERTAINLY TOOK YOUR SWEET TIME.
THIS CAGE SMELLS SUSPICIOUS.
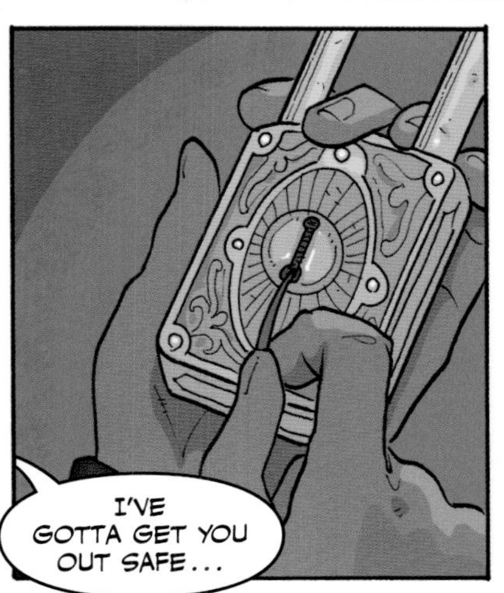
I'VE GOTTA GET YOU OUT SAFE...

...AND GO HELP PUNZIE.

WATCH YOURSELF THEN.

MOMMA, I'M SORRY. I'VE FAILED YOU MY WHOLE LIFE.

NO, NO, YOU WERE GROWING UP, IS ALL. I LOVE YOU, JACK. I LOVE YOU SOMETHING FIERCE.

I'M BETTING MY CLEVER SON HAS A PLAN FOR GETTING ME OUT OF THIS TILTING SKY BOAT.
And you know what? I did!

THE BLUNDERBOAR BUILDING, IT'S YOURS NOW, OR WHAT'LL BE LEFT OF IT AFTER THAT MOB CHASES THE GIANTS OUT. BLUNDERBOAR AGREED, YOU HEARD HIM. THE WHOLE CITY HEARD.

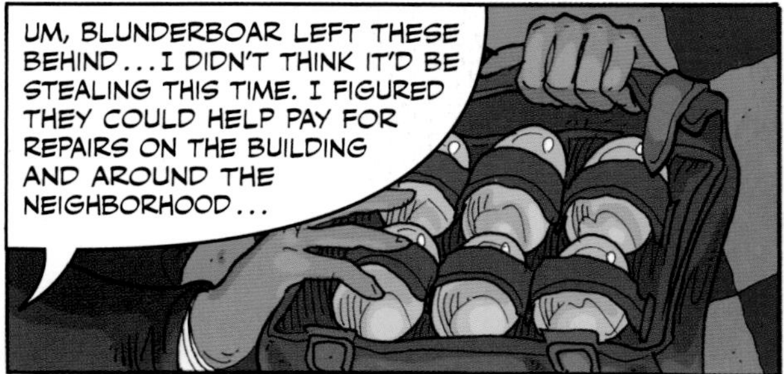
UM, BLUNDERBOAR LEFT THESE BEHIND... I DIDN'T THINK IT'D BE STEALING THIS TIME. I FIGURED THEY COULD HELP PAY FOR REPAIRS ON THE BUILDING AND AROUND THE NEIGHBORHOOD...

AND BUY A SHE-GOAT BESIDES, I'D WAGER.

MOMMA, I JUST WANT YOU TO KNOW, I'M DONE WITH THE STEALING AND SCHEMING. FOREVER. I'M ONE OF THE GOOD GUYS.

YES, YOU ARE. YOUR POPPA WOULD BE PROUD.
She touched my cheek and something inside me slid back into place. Something broken didn't hurt anymore.

HERE'S ONE FOR LUCK.
GIVE THAT BRUTE WHAT-FOR FROM YOUR MOMMA!

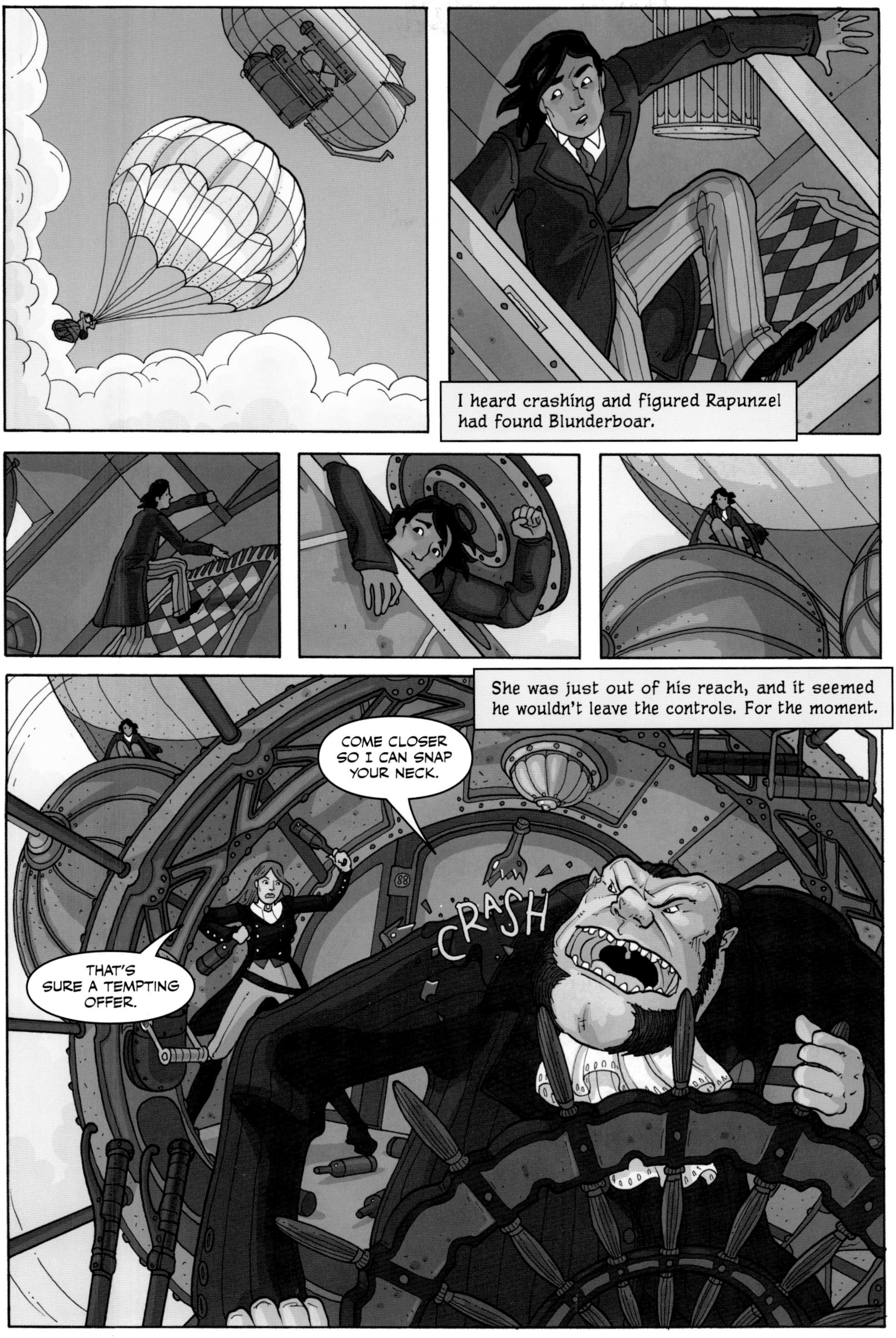

She was just out of his reach, and it seemed he wouldn't leave the controls. For the moment.

COME CLOSER SO I CAN SNAP YOUR NECK.

CRASH

THAT'S SURE A TEMPTING OFFER.

INSTEAD, WHY DON'T YOU LET ME TAKE THE WHEEL SO I CAN TIP THIS SHIP OVER AND SEND YOU SPRAWLING TO YOUR DOOM?

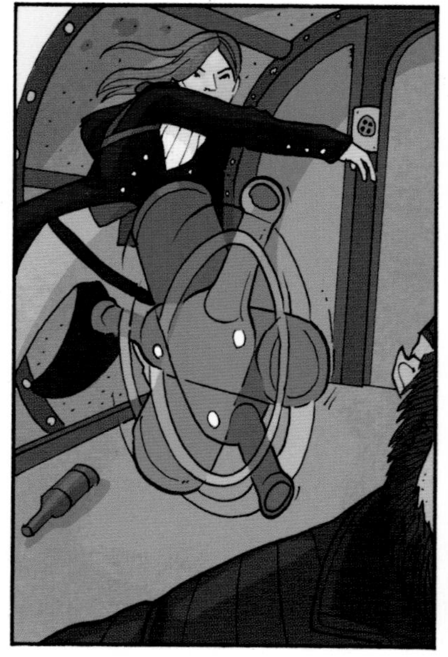

SNAP

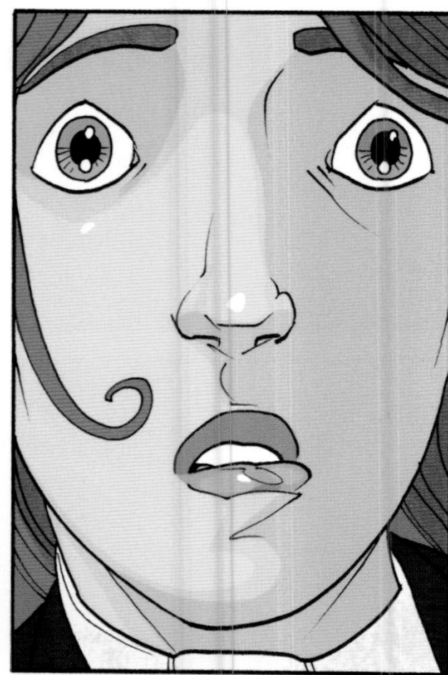

CRAK

STAY PUT WHILE I HARNESS THE WHEEL...
...SO I CAN TOSS *YOU* TO YOUR DOOM.

No. No! Think, Jack, think.

CRASH
HEY, BONEHEAD!

WHAT!? HOW THE DEVIL...

THE GOOSE-
HER EGGS AREN'T JUST GOLDEN-
THEY'RE MAGIC.

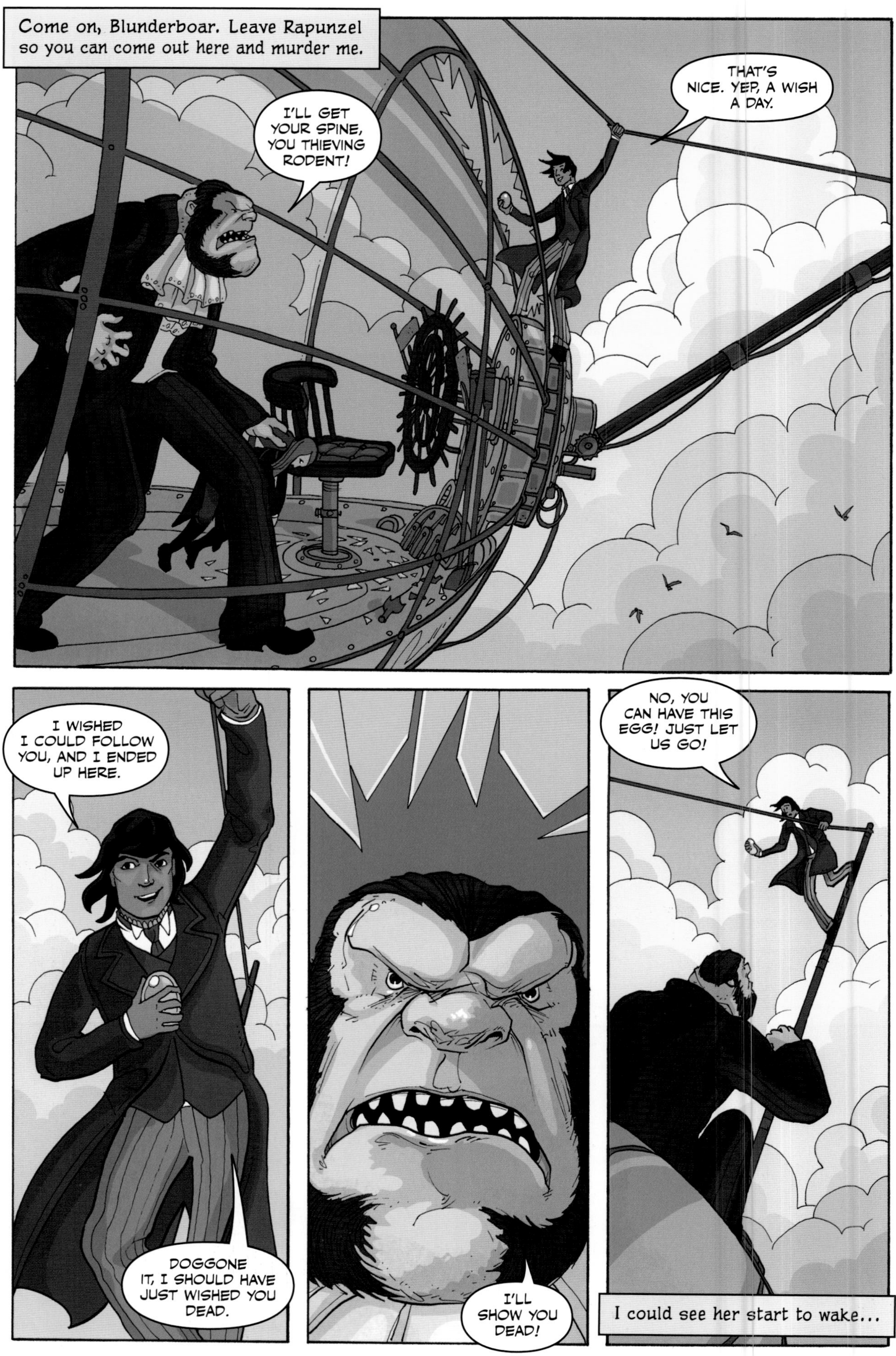

Come on, Blunderboar. Leave Rapunzel so you can come out here and murder me.

I'LL GET YOUR SPINE, YOU THIEVING RODENT!

THAT'S NICE. YEP, A WISH A DAY.

I could see her start to wake...

I had to keep the oaf distracted...
HERE! JUST TAKE IT!

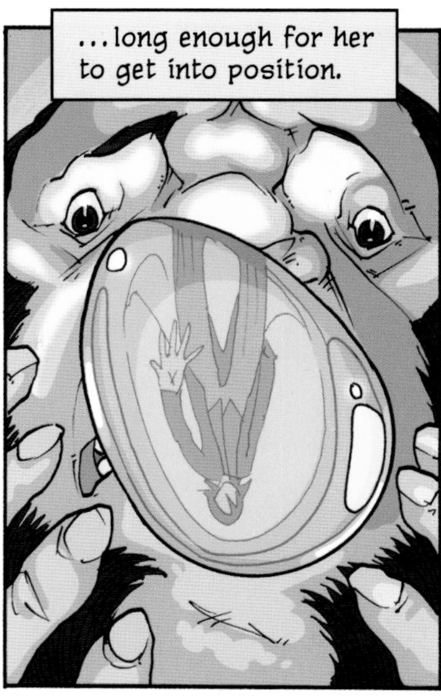

...long enough for her to get into position.

I WISH YOU DEAD.

Not the best of signals, but I knew she'd understand.

My Punzie.

As smart as they come.

IT'S A SHAME HOW YOU JUST CAN'T TRUST MAGIC THESE DAYS.

I WISH YOU DEAD!

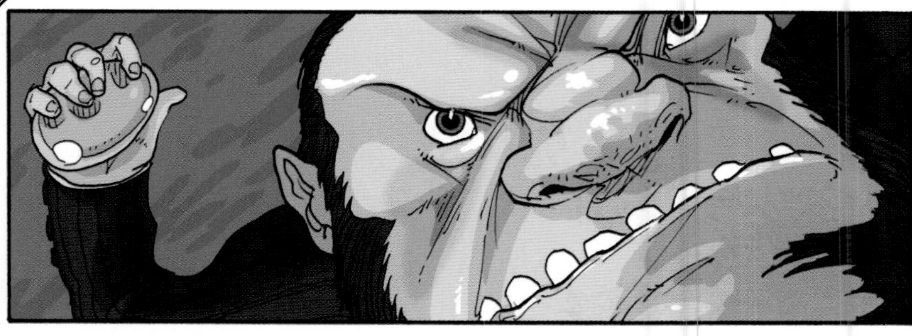

SNAP

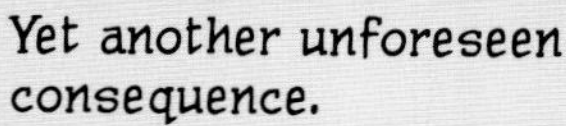

Yet another unforeseen consequence.

CREEEEAK
But who would've guessed Mr. Frilly Shirt had that kind of pitching arm?

SLAM

YAAAAAH!

No.

No!
SNAP

YAAAAH!
Lucky Blunderboar weighed so much more than me. The pulley was bringing me up fast.

FFFFFFFFFFFFFFF
Too fast.

KRAK KRAK

HOLD ON THERE, MISTER.

LOOKS LIKE HE LANDED IN THE OCEAN. MAYBE HE'LL SWIM BACK TO THE OLD WORLD, UNLESS...
...ARE THOSE SHARKS?
LOOKS LIKE. STILL, BLUNDERBOAR'S PRETTY WILY. MAYBE HE'LL SWEET-TALK THE SHARK LEADERS AND ENSLAVE THE WHOLE OCEAN.

OR MAYBE THEY'LL JUST EAT HIM. GIANT BONES DO WONDERS FOR A SHARK'S HEALTH.

OKAY. I THINK I CAN GET IT TO TURN AROUND, BUT THE WHOLE UP-DOWN PART IS A MYSTERY.

HEY, THINK THIS OMNIPHONE WORKS UP HERE?
...AGAIN, THIS IS FREDERICK SPARKSMITH THE THIRD REPORTING FROM THE FORMER HEADQUARTERS OF BLUNDERBOAR AND COMPANY. THINGS ARE WRAPPING UP PRETTY AS A PRESENT.
THERE'S THE MAYOR AND HIS PEOPLE TAKING STATEMENTS FROM ALL THE GIANTS WHO DIDN'T FLEE. THEY'RE BEING PARDONED IF THEY AGREE TO HELP REBUILD THE BUSINESSES THAT WERE DAMAGED IN THIS SO-CALLED WAR.

IF YOU CAN HEAR MUSIC, THERE'S A RATHER IMPRESSIVE CELEBRATION IN THE STREET IN HONOR OF MY FRIENDS JACK AND RAPUNZEL. YOU DID IT, FRIENDS! BINGO! THAT IS, I MEAN TO SAY, YEE-HA!

GUESS WE SHOULD FIGURE OUT A WAY TO GET BACK. THERE'S BOUND TO BE LOVELY GIRLS IN THAT ADORING CROWD HOPING TO KISS THE HERO...
AND I GUESS YOU'D LIKE TO LEAP INTO FREDDIE'S ARMS.

LISTEN, I DON'T CARE IF HE'S SO RICH HE WIPES WITH PAPER MONEY AND HAS THE WHOLE "HANDSOME" THING GOING ON.
YOU'RE MY GAL, RAPUNZEL, AND I'M NOT JUST GOING TO FALL DOWN WITHOUT A FIGHT, GOT IT?
FREDDIE?
JACK...

WHAT? WHAT? YOU DON'T THINK I CAN TAKE HIM?
SOMETIMES YOUR HEAD DOES A GOOD IMITATION OF A HARD-BOILED EGG.

SO, YOU DON'T FANCY FREDDIE...
UM...I PICKED UP SOMETHING FOR YOU BACK AT BLUNDERBOAR'S.

IT'S NOT MUCH, BUT PRU SAID...NEVER MIND. NOTHING'S GONE RIGHT. I WAS SUPPOSED TO COME HOME AND BUILD A NEW TENEMENT AND BAKERY...
...AND YOU'D SEE HOW CITIFIED AND SLICK I AM AND, YOU KNOW, ADMIRE ME, MORE OR LESS, 'CAUSE I...I... NEVER MIND, THIS WAS A STUPID–

NO, IT'S NICE, I WANT IT.
THANKS. I...
Tears? Not quite the reaction I'd hoped for.

UH, YOU OKAY, PUNZIE?
YES, I JUST– I DIDN'T THINK YOU LIKED ME, YOU KNOW, LIKE THAT, ANYMORE.

THAT'S BECAUSE I'VE BEEN A RIGHT NUMBSKULL.
THAT'S ABOUT THE SWEETEST THING YOU'VE EVER SAID. I HAVE SOMETHING FOR YOU, TOO.

MY POPPA'S... YOU FOUND THIS? BUT WHEN?
YOU GUYS WERE BUSY MAKING THE TRAP, SO I–

HOW DID YOU FIND THE PAWNSHOP?
I LISTENED WHEN YOU TALKED ABOUT IT, FIGURED SOME STUFF OUT, CROSSED MY FINGERS IT WAS STILL THERE. PRETTY GOOD FOR A BACKWATER GAL, HUH?

PRETTY GREAT. THIS IS... THIS IS...